THREAD OF FATE

Ejine Okoroafor

© Copyright 2024 by Ejine Okoroafor. All rights reserved.

No part of this work may be reproduced, distributed, stored in a retrieval system, or transmitted in any form or by any means—whether electronic, mechanical, photocopying, recording, or otherwise—without the prior written permission of the author, except in the case of brief quotations embodied in critical articles or reviews. Any unauthorized use of this work is strictly prohibited and may result in legal action.

This is a work of fiction. All characters, names, events, locations, organizations, and dialogues within this novel are purely products of the author's imagination or are used fictitiously. Any resemblance to actual persons, living or deceased, or real events is entirely coincidental. The author assumes no responsibility for interpretations or implications drawn from the fictional content of this work.

Here's to the beauty of sisterhood and bonds that lift us higher!

Dedicated to the sisterhoods and bonds, whether through the ties of birth or the sacred connection of friendship, form an unbreakable circle of support, laughter, and shared dreams.

PROEM

Adaobi's story had us all leaning in, completely captivated. Her words had that magnetic pull, the kind that could draw you in and make you forget everything else. It was not just the story itself but the way she told it—animated, full of life, and with that hint of suspense that kept you hanging on every word.

Clara, despite the discomfort from her recent myomectomy, was perched on the edge of her seat, her eyes wide with interest. Ikunnu, ever the skeptic, wore a knowing smile, while Ifeyinwa and Chinelo exchanged glances that were a mix of amusement and anticipation.

The room, filled with the scent of Clara's freshly brewed tea and the soft hum of old school memories, felt almost sacred—a sanctuary of their shared past and present.

"So, did he live up to the voice?" Chinelo finally broke the silence, her tone teasing but curious. Her question was one we all wanted the answer to.

Adaobi's eyes sparkled with that familiar mischievous glint as she leaned back in her chair, taking her time. We knew she was savoring this moment, the attention squarely on her, the anticipation building in the air.

"I swear that I had arrived early enough to hear his flight details announced when the plane touched down," Adaobi began again, her voice tinged with excitement. "I was that eager to meet Okechukwu. I mean, from the moment Eze told me about him, something just... sparked. But it was his voice that really got me."

She paused, letting the weight of her words settle. "Did I even mention that his voice was one of the most enchanting voices I've ever heard? It was rich, deep, and oh, so smooth. The kind of voice that could make you feel all sorts of things with just one word."

We all nodded, picturing it, feeling the slight chill she described as if we had heard it ourselves.

"When Eze initially asked if he could pass my number to his cousin, Okechukwu, I hesitated. You know how skeptical I am about those types of things. I didn't want to be dragged into any 'arrange ...eee wedding o.'" Adaobi jokingly drawled while laughing and mimicking her own wary tone.

We chuckled along, knowing exactly what she meant.

"But Eze was persistent," she continued, her expression softening. "He kept insisting that we would make a good match, and that Okechukwu wasn't your 'typical Nigerian.'"

Ikunnu couldn't resist interjecting, "What is typical Nigerian?" she asked, feigning indignation, though we all knew the answer could be endless.

Adaobi waved her off playfully. "I'm afraid you'd have to ask Eze o." Her laughter was infectious, and we all joined in.

She paused again, her eyes momentarily drifting as if she was lost in memory. "Anyway, when Okechukwu finally called, I was pleasantly surprised to hear his smooth, deep baritone voice. As they say, 'He had me from hello!' And from then on, I became a prayer warrior. I prayed for his personality to match with his rich voice."

We all burst into laughter at the absurdity of it, but there was something endearing about her honesty. Only Adaobi would turn something like that into a prayer point.

"But that's not all," Adaobi continued, leaning in conspiratorially, her voice dropping to a near whisper.

We all quieted down; our curiosity piqued even further. There was more to this story, more than just a voice, and we were all eager to find out what it was.

And just like that, she had us right where she wanted us—completely engrossed, hanging on to every word, and utterly captivated by the tale that was unfolding. This was only the beginning, and whatever came next, we were ready, eager to soak in every detail of Adaobi's enchanting story. She had a way of spinning tales that left you on the edge of your seat, waiting for the next twist or unexpected punchline.

"The first sign of trouble was after he emailed me his picture. I wasn't exactly taken by it," Adaobi confessed, her voice dropping slightly as if sharing a secret. She leaned forward, her expression a mix of amusement and something else—maybe disappointment, maybe disbelief.

"Unlike his voice, he looked particularly Nigerian." She laughed, but there was a hint of something more in her tone, a blend of humor and resignation.

"Wait o, you know you aren't getting away with that one!" Ikunnu jumped in, refusing to let her off the hook with such a vague statement. "You must clarify this your 'particularly Nigerian' or 'not' statements o!"

Adaobi rolled her eyes playfully, clearly enjoying the attention. "Oh, c'mon, Ikunnu, you know what I mean," she said, as if that explained everything.

But Ikunnu wasn't about to let it slide.

"I don't know about the others, but I do not know what you mean," Ikunnu insisted, feigning seriousness as she folded her arms and leaned in, waiting for Adaobi to dig herself out of this one.

"Yes ooo, we need explanations on that one," Ifeyinwa concurred, backing her up with a grin.

We all loved to tease Adaobi, especially when she gets flustered over her latest romantic escapade. Her cheeks would flush, and she'd roll her eyes dramatically, but you could always tell she secretly enjoyed the attention.

Adaobi sighed dramatically, as if the weight of our demands was too much for her to bear.

"Okay, okay, well, you know the typical Nigerian—or rather Igbo man—is assumed to be very autocratic, expecting a submissive wife.

The kind of woman who will ask, 'How high?' when he asks her to jump," she explained, her tone a mix of jest and a touch of truth.

"Okay ooo," Ifeyinwa nodded as if that cleared things up, though the smirk on her face told a different story. "But you still haven't explained the 'particularly Nigerian' look."

Adaobi hesitated, clearly trying to find the right words.

"Well... you know... some men just have that... I don't know... that look, that aura. It's hard to explain," she stammered, clearly realizing she was digging herself deeper. "But it's not always a bad thing! It's just... a thing."

"Oh, you're not getting away with that non-answer," Chinelo retorted, still grinning, enjoying how flustered Adaobi was getting.

"Just drop it, Chi..., we all know what she means," Clara interjected, her voice gently chiding Chinelo but with a smile.

Clara had always been the peacemaker among us, the one who knew when to move things along.

Adaobi seized the opportunity to continue, clearly relieved to steer the conversation back to safer ground.

"Anyway," she resumed, "I refused to let his looks put me off. If his face didn't match that voice, maybe his personality would."

"Oh, I think I remember him now. You sounded really excited about the prospects of your meeting," Ifeyinwa recalled, her eyes narrowing slightly as she connected the dots.

"Yes o, and I really was," Adaobi confirmed with a wistful sigh. "We talked endlessly on the phone. I'd hurry to finish my chores after work or during the weekends, just so I could lie in bed, listening and drooling over that voice when he called. I even started considering that he might be 'the one.'" She emphasized the last part with a dramatic wriggle of her fingers beside her ears, as if quoting some romantic movie line.

"Okay, okay," Chinelo urged eagerly, barely able to contain her curiosity. "So, what happened?"

Adaobi's expression turned mischievous; the kind of look that said she had something good up her sleeve. "I forgot to mention that I had momentarily contemplated carrying a placard with his name on it like they do at airports, but I chickened out at the last minute. I wasn't sure if he'd get the joke," she admitted with a chuckle, clearly enjoying the image of herself as some sort of rom-com heroine.

"Anyhow, I jostled my way to the front row as a new wave of passengers made their way out to the arrival's hall. I was so eager to see if I could spot him as he walked out. Soon enough, there he was."

"Yes…?" we all echoed, hanging on to her every word.

"I was a bit taken aback to see him awkwardly pushing a trolley laden with suitcases. I mean, he was flying from Atlanta for a few days, right?"

"I'm not sure where you're going with that one," Ifeyinwa interjected, unimpressed by the detail. "He might have loads of presents for you."

"Well, that's possible, but no," Adaobi shook her head, her expression growing more serious. "I'm still on the matter of how he was pushing that trolley. As he drew nearer, and I could clearly see his entire frame, I noticed that his bum was crooked."

"His bum was crooked." Chinelo repeated, incredulous, as the image she was painting became even more puzzling. What on earth was Adaobi talking about?

"Yes, crooked," Adaobi affirmed, nodding earnestly. "He was walking with his hips held up at a rather odd angle." She stood up, her face deadly serious as she demonstrated, arms outstretched, hips tilted awkwardly to one side and proceeded to mimic his gait with a slight limp.

"Look, he was walking this way."

We all erupted in laughter, tears streaming down our faces as we tried to imagine this man and Adaobi's reaction. The way she was demonstrating, so deadpan yet so animated, only made it funnier.

But Adaobi's expression remained resolute, determined to make us understand.

"Right there and then I knew," she declared, her voice firm. "I just couldn't envisage spending my whole life with him."

"That was it?" Chinelo countered, both mystified and unconvinced.

"Just like that?"

"Yes, that was it, and another one bit the dust!" Adaobi concluded in a sing-song voice, prior to bursting into laughter as she finished with a mock bow and threw her hands in the air in mock jubilation.

Adaobi's laughter echoed around the room, but it didn't spark the usual chorus of giggles from the rest. Instead, a heavy silence settled in, and Chinelo could see the confusion flicker across her face. They exchanged glances, silently communicating their shared concern.

"Don't you get the funny side?" Adaobi asked, her brows knitting together in genuine bafflement. The playful spark in her eyes dimmed as she looked at each of them.

"No," Ikunnu responded bluntly, setting down her glass of water with a soft clink. "To be honest, I think you're taking this pickiness of yours a bit too far."

Adaobi blinked, clearly taken aback by her straightforwardness.

"But I just didn't like the angle of his butt," she protested, her voice slipping into a childish whine. "No offense, but his gait reminded me of those market women back home, awkwardly lugging heavy logs of firewood on their heads."

"I still don't get your point," Chinelo countered, refusing to let her off the hook. "Remember the other time? You were turned off by how another guy held his fork or cutlery at dinner. Are we supposed to take this seriously?"

"Really?" Ifeyinwa interjected, half-jokingly but with an unmistakable glint of amusement. "Those aren't even her worst excuses! Remember that dashing American guy who came home while we were still in Nigeria? Adaobi got disenchanted with him because instead of giving her a pack of his prized 'BIG RED' chewing gum, he kept offering her just a piece a time, like she was a kid."

Ifeyinwa's recounting of the story sparked laughter from the group. It was as if they weren't ready to let Adaobi escape the scrutiny.

"I remember that one, but I think the most ridiculous was the guy with the runs on their first date," Clara added.

"Oh my God, I do remember that one too!" Chinelo's eyes widened with glee as she chimed in. "And he left the toilet door open while doing his business!"

"He was offering you the full experience, sound effects and all," Clara quipped, her eyes twinkling as they all burst into laughter again.

Adaobi covered her face, laughing along but shaking her head. "I wanted to vanish right there! The worst part is, he acted like it was totally normal!"

"If that's normal, I don't want to know what weird is," Chinelo said, barely able to hold her laughter.

Adaobi, though clearly starting to feel a bit defensive, tried to justify herself.

"C'mon, you wouldn't call me shallow for that, would you?"

"Okay, okay, we'll let you off the hook for that one," Clara conceded, her tone softening. "He was totally gross. But on a more serious note, what exactly are you looking for? Mr. Perfect?"

"Far from it," Adaobi protested, her tone more serious now. "I'm just following my instincts. I'm not stupid. You all know me better than that."

"We do," Clara replied, her concern clear. "Which is why we're worried. Time isn't on our side anymore. We want to see you happily married and settled, like the rest of us. Maybe it's time to rethink your priorities." She paused, then added more gently, "But that's just my two cents."

"I remember someone once saying that if you don't like someone, any excuse becomes a good excuse," Chinelo offered, her tone lighter as she tried to ease the tension. She reached over and patted Adaobi's hand. "The point is, Adaobi just didn't like those fellows!" She put on an exaggerated American accent, drawing more laughter.

"True," they all agreed in unison.

"Okay, you guys had me worried there for a moment," Adaobi admitted with a small sigh of relief. "I thought you'd all lost your sense of humor. Look, I was just making light of my encounters for comic effect. It's not as simple as I made it sound, but the bottom line is, I didn't really like any of those guys."

Clara nodded, her expression thoughtful. "We understand, and I'm sure you know what's best for you. But we're concerned because time is ticking. The biological clock is real, and none of us is getting any younger. I hope you're prioritizing the right things because, trust me, when you're married, how your husband handles his fork will be the least of your worries."

"Clara's right," Chinelo agreed with a sigh, her voice carrying the weight of experience. "Marriage isn't easy, but like everything else in life, if you really want it, you have to work at it."

"You're both right," Adaobi responded thoughtfully. "Don't get me wrong, I don't have any grand illusions about marriage. Although, I'll admit, those Mills & Boon novels we read back in the day might suggest otherwise," she added with a mischievous grin, drawing chuckles from us all. "But I do need to choose someone I genuinely like and love. It'll make the journey more bearable. And trust me, I've learned a lot from you guys."

"True," they all murmured, the atmosphere growing more reflective as the conversation took on a deeper tone.

Chinelo glanced at her watch and sighed, reaching for her bag. "I need to head home before Osi gets back."

"Has he changed?" Clara asked softly, her voice tinged with concern.

"No," Chinelo replied, her face a mask of quiet resignation. "He's still the same. I've accepted that he's my cross to bear. These days, I must be extra careful—never sure what will set him off. It's like walking on hot coals."

"It is well, my sister," Clara said, her hand resting on Chinelo's shoulder in a gesture of comfort. "Just remember, we're here for you."

"I know," Chinelo replied, her voice softening as she looked around at them. "Who would've thought, back in school, that we'd all end up living in the United States, and so close to each other in New York and New Jersey of all places?"

"I know," Ifeyinwa agreed, her voice warm with nostalgia. "But God works in mysterious ways. And the best part of this journey is that we're all together here, supporting each other."

"True," Clara nodded, "though we always knew Adaobi would return to the States. But for the rest of us? This," she gestured around the room, "this was just a dream."

"We're living the American dream," Chinelo said with a mock bow, causing more laughter amongst the group, the heaviness of the earlier conversation lifting as they embraced the joy of their shared experiences.

In that moment, as the laughter echoed around the room, Chinelo felt a deep sense of gratitude. They had come so far—from their college days at their alma mater, University of Port-Harcourt or UniPort in Nigeria to this living room in New York City. Life had taken them on different paths, but somehow, they had found their way back to each other and to the present time.

Looking around at Clara, Adaobi, Ikunnu and Ifeyinwa, Chinelo marveled at how much they had all changed. The wild dreams of their youth had evolved into hard-earned realities, marked by heartbreak, success, motherhood, and marriages, both failed and flourishing. Yet, through it all, this sisterhood had still been a constant, their shared history a reminder of who they were and how far they had come.

As Chinelo stood to leave, the mood was light but filled with the camaraderie that only years of friendship could build.

"My dears, I love you all, but I think I'll depart with Chinelo," Adaobi announced, gathering her things. Turning to Chinelo, she added,

"And Chi dear, please can you drop me off at any Metro in the Bronx please."

"Of course, Nnem," Chinelo assured her, using the affectionate Igbo term for "girlfriend" for Adaobi as she smiled warmly, while Adaobi, intermittently called her by the short form of her name, Chi.

The bond between them had always felt more like family than friendship.

"Let's go then," Chinelo urged, giving her a playful nudge as they stood up together.

The five women trooped to the door, helping Adaobi and Chinelo with their bags. Laughter and light chatter filled the air as they made their way outside, the cool evening breeze brushing against their faces. They proceeded to Chinelo's car parked on the busy street, the ever-present hustle and bustle of New York City serving as a constant backdrop—car horns blaring, people weaving through sidewalks, and the faint sound of street vendors calling out their last sales of the night.

Clara glanced around and sighed contentedly. "I still can't believe we're all here, together, in this city."

"Feels like a lifetime ago we were back at UniPort," Ifeyinwa mused, her eyes scanning the tall buildings as they reached the car.

Chinelo popped the trunk and smiled. "And yet, here we are. Different city, same sisterhood."

Adaobi chuckled, tossing her bag inside. "Who would've thought? From Port-Harcourt to this madness. Life is wild."

"Wild, but good," Clara added, linking arms with Chinelo.

"Thanks again, ladies, for dropping by. I know how many times we've planned a formal reunion without being able to make it all at the same time. I'm so grateful you could all come today. We talk regularly on the phone, but nothing beats meeting up in person," Clara said, her voice warm with appreciation.

"You're right. We should really try to meet up more often," Ifeyinwa suggested.

"Yes, and maybe take an all-girls holiday trip together at some point in the future," Clara proposed, her eyes lighting up at the idea.

"Lovely idea," echoed Adaobi. "Count me in anytime, you guys are the ones with the extra baggage," she joked, gesturing playfully at the others with spouses, kids or both.

"You can say that again, Nnem," Chinelo chimed in. "But we can still plan, right? They say that where there's a will, there's a way."

"And where there's a saying, there's our proverbial Chinelo," Clara quipped dryly, drawing laughter from the others.

"That's what happens when you're raised by an informed grandmother who constantly explained life in adages," Chinelo retorted with a grin.

"There's nothing wrong with that either," Ifeyinwa reassured her. "I remember your grandma, Inem Akpara. She was such a strong and fiery old lady."

"Are you kidding me? She sure was," Chinelo agreed. "I miss her daily. I wish I could have been able to pick her brains on my present predicament."

"Never mind, dear," Clara said, patting her on the shoulder. "She would have been proud of the fine lady that you are. She raised you right, which is why you've been able to conduct yourself with utmost dignity and patience in the face of your present predicament. I commend you."

"Thanks, ladies, for all your support." Chinelo said with a hint of emotion, before turning to Adaobi. "Okay oh, Adaobi, we must really go."

The group shared another round of hugs and kisses on their cheeks, lingering in the warmth of their closeness. Adaobi and Chinelo finally climbed into the car, the door closing with a soft thud that seemed to signal the end of a perfect evening.

As they pulled away from the curb, Clara, Ikunnu, and Ifeyinwa stood together on the steps of Clara's home, waving them off with wide smiles. They watched as the car's taillights disappeared into the flow of traffic. Clara glanced at her two friends by her side and sighed happily.

"It's always hard to say goodbye." "If we didn't have to adult so much, we'd be having sleepovers and midnight talks like we used to," Ikunnu joked, giving Clara a nudge.

"If only," Ifeyinwa smiled, tucking a loose strand of hair behind her ear. "But tonight reminded me we'll always make time for each other, no matter what."

Clara nodded, her heart full. "That's what matters.

CHINELO

As Chinelo and Adaobi drove off, the mood in the car shifted slightly. The laughter and warmth from earlier lingered, but the reality of New York City traffic soon set in. The streets were thick with cars, barely crawling forward as horns blared impatiently from all directions. Pedestrians darted across the road with little regard for the crosswalks, adding to the chaos.

"New York, huh?" Adaobi muttered, shaking her head as she watched someone jaywalk just inches from the car's front bumper.

Chinelo sighed, gripping the wheel tighter. "Every time I think I've seen the worst of it, the city finds a way to remind me I haven't."

They inched forward, navigating through the congested streets with care. The once lighthearted atmosphere felt more subdued, as both women focused on the road ahead.

"You know," Adaobi began, her tone quieter now, "I'm really glad we did this today. I didn't realize how much I needed it until we were all together again."

Chinelo glanced over for a moment, then back to the road. "Yeah, me too. It's crazy how life pulls us in different directions, but when we get back together, it's like nothing has changed."

Adaobi smiled, leaning back in her seat. "Except for the traffic. That always changes. And somehow, it's always worse."

Chinelo laughed, shaking her head. "You're not wrong about that."

"Our Clara is such a strong lady; she's already up and about. It's like her fifth day following her fibroid surgery, and she's as good as if nothing had happened," Adaobi commented, glancing out the window as they approached a red light.

"Tell me about it. I hope she takes this chance to rest rather than perpetually waiting hand and foot on her beloved Emeka," Chinelo replied, while trying to keep her focus on the chaotic road ahead.

Just then, a yellow New York City taxi cut in front of them, forcing her to brake suddenly.

"Honestly, this traffic is a nightmare." Adaobi commented, prior to returning to their conversation. "It's not like you said it but it's almost like Clara would say, "how high", if Emeka would ask her to jump."

"Yes, oh, Nnem, but at least Emeka doesn't beat Clara up." Chinelo pointed out, her tone turning serious.

"True," Adaobi agreed, her voice heavy with concern. "I'll be lying if I say I'm not disturbed by your situation with Osi. I still can't get my head around the fact that the same quiet and amiable Osi, who one would ordinarily deem incapable of hurting a fly, turns out to be a vicious wife beater."

Chinelo sighed, staring out at the gridlocked traffic as they finally merged onto I-678N, heading toward the Van Wyck Expressway.

"I know, Nnem. It's like living with a stranger, someone I thought I knew, but who's become someone else entirely." Chinelo commented while carefully maneuvering the car through the thick traffic.

Adaobi was silent for a moment, "You don't deserve this, Chinelo. None of us do."

"I just have to be extra careful these days, you know? I can never be sure of what will set him off. It's literally like threading on thin ice or walking on hot coals," Chinelo confessed, her voice barely above a whisper. "I don't even know which of those is worse."

"It is well, my sister," Adaobi said softly, reaching over to give her friend's hand a reassuring squeeze. "Just remember that we're here for you, always."

"I know," Chinelo replied, a small, sad smile playing on her face.

"But I sometimes wonder how things got this bad. Who could have predicted back when we were in school that we'd all end up living in New York and nearby New Jersey, facing our own different battles?"

"I know," Adaobi nodded, thinking about how life had taken them on such unexpected journeys. "But God surely works in mysterious ways."

"And that we're all together here is the best part of this journey, and for a good cause," Ifeyinwa's earlier words echoed in Chinelo's mind.

Chinelo's car swerved sharply, tires squealing as she narrowly avoided the motorcyclist who had recklessly cut in front of her without a second thought. The blare of horns echoed through the chaotic streets, mingling with the constant hum of New York City traffic.

"Onye ala! Madman!" Chinelo cursed under her breath, her pulse still racing as she regained control of the car, her knuckles white as she gripped the steering wheel. The relentless pace of the city was nothing compared to the wild, unpredictable roads back home, but it still brought out the same instinctual reactions.

Adaobi, who had been momentarily lost in her thoughts, was jolted back to reality by the sudden movement. She steadied herself, letting out a nervous laugh.

"Chi, it seems like motorcyclists are a universal nuisance," she said, her voice tinged with a mix of relief and exasperation.

Chinelo shook her head, still seething from the narrow escape.

"They sure are. The way they appear out of nowhere—like phantoms in the night—it's a miracle we don't knock them over more often. You have to be on guard all the time."

Adaobi sighed deeply, her thoughts drifting back to familiar memories. "There's no difference between them and our own unique motorcyclists, *okada* back home," she said, her tone wistful.

Chinelo couldn't help but smile, the tension easing as nostalgia crept in.

"True, but I have to say, the *okada* riders back home are in a league of their own. They're everywhere, and they drive those battered motorcycles like they're invincible, without so much as a helmet or a second thought. Remember when we lived in Lagos? I refused to drive outside Lagos Island. The mainland was just too chaotic for me. I wasn't built for that kind of madness."

Adaobi's eyes sparkled with shared memories, her laughter softening the seriousness that had been weighing on her.

"I don't blame you one bit. Those okada riders were a menace, but driving in Nigeria is an entirely different kind of survival game. I remember those scorching hot afternoons, stuck in traffic on the Third Mainland Bridge. The heat, the frustration—it could turn the calmest person into a reckless driver. You'd just squeeze in anywhere you could, horns blaring, no rules, just instinct. If you couldn't beat them, you joined them. Ah, those were the days."

The two women erupted into laughter, the memories of their past adventures chasing away the remnants of tension. The city outside their windows blurred as they sped along, the laughter a soothing balm over the rough edges of their day.

But as the laughter faded, a shadow fell over Chinelo's face. Her thoughts returned to her husband, Osi, and the troubles that had been gnawing at her heart. She sighed, the weight of her worries evident in her voice.

"But honestly, Adaobi, things with Osi... they're not what they used to be. I know this isn't the man I married. It's like something dark has taken hold of him, something beyond my understanding. He's changed so much since our circumstances took a turn. At first, I thought he was just frustrated, lashing out because of our situation, but now... when he's in one of those moods, it's like he's possessed.

His eyes, Adaobi... they're different. He looks at me like I'm a stranger, like I'm the enemy."

Adaobi's heart ached for her friend, sensing the depth of her pain.

"Oh, Chinelo, I can't imagine what you're going through. But I remember how you and Osi were back then, so in love, so inseparable. You were the couple everyone envied, the lovebirds of UniPort. I know things are hard now, but I believe it will get better. You two have something special."

Chinelo's smile was weak, more an attempt to convince herself than Adaobi.

"I remember those days too, Nnem. The early days at UniPort when we first met. We were so young, so in love, so wrapped up in each other. It felt like nothing could ever come between us. We just knew we were meant to be together for life. That's why we got married so soon after graduation. It's hard to believe it's only been six years, but it feels like a lifetime. I used to dream of having a man who was completely into me, who couldn't get enough of me. But now... it's suffocating. It's true what they say, be careful what you pray for."

Adaobi reached over, squeezing Chinelo's hand in solidarity.

"It's true, Chinelo, but you've always been a storyteller, weaving these little nuggets of wisdom into everything."

Chinelo laughed, though there was a bittersweet note in it.

"Blame my grandma. She had a way of making life seem like one big story, full of lessons and warnings."

Adaobi smiled caringly, her heart full of affection for her friend.

"And that's what I love about you. No matter what, you always find a way to see the bigger picture. I know things are tough right now, but keep the faith, Chinelo. You and Osi have been through too much together to let this tear you apart."

Chinelo sighed deeply, a mix of gratitude and lingering worry in her eyes.

"Thanks, Adaobi. I just hope you're right. I really do."

The skyscrapers of New York loomed above, casting long shadows as the sun began to dip in the sky as they continued their journey. Chinelo continued navigating through the traffic with practiced ease, her attention divided between the road and telling Adaobi her story.

"I had to curb most of those bad driving habits that we picked up back home after moving here," Chinelo mused, a hint of nostalgia in her voice. "It's almost unbelievable now, thinking about the stunts we used to pull on the roads back in Nigeria. I mean, who in their right mind would think it's normal to squeeze a car through a gap meant for a motorcycle?"

Adaobi chuckled, her eyes flicking to the rearview mirror. "I know, right? If we tried even half of those maneuvers here, the NYPD would have us in handcuffs before we could say 'I'm sorry, officer.'"

Chinelo grinned, shaking her head.

"The po-po! I remember the first time I heard someone call them that—I nearly died of laughter. It's like something straight out of a Madea movie!"

"The po-po," Adaobi echoed, laughing. "Madea would be proud of us."

Their laughter bubbled up, filling the car with a lightness that only old friends could share. As the city's rhythm pulsed around them, Chinelo's gaze drifted out the window, her thoughts taking a more reflective turn.

"You know what really surprised me on my first visit to New York?" she began, her voice softening as she stared out at the skyline. "It was the parks and harbors. I had always pictured New York as this concrete jungle, all skyscrapers and busy streets. But then I saw the greenery, the parks, the trees lining the highways, and the rivers that thread through the city. It was nothing like what I had imagined."

Adaobi nodded, a smile playing on her lips as she caught the wistfulness in Chinelo's voice.

"New York is a beautiful city, no doubt about it. It reminds me of Lagos in some ways, with its islands and mainland, but with a bit more order and structure. Central Park is my favorite—especially in spring when the flowers are in bloom, fewer tourists, and the city feels like it's coming alive."

Chinelo raised an eyebrow, a playful glint in her eyes. "Fewer tourists, you say? Central Park, like Times Square, is always teeming with people, no matter the season."

Adaobi laughed, conceding. "Okay, okay, maybe not fewer tourists, but there's something about spring that makes it feel a little less crowded, don't you think?"

"Perhaps," Chinelo agreed, her smile fading slightly as she returned to her story. "Anyway, as I was saying, Osi and I got married right after our youth service. My dear Osita—his full name, not just Osi like I usually call him—secured a job with the Ministry of Works, and I was lucky enough to be retained by Union Bank, where I had served. We rented a modest one-bedroom flat and started to build our life together."

Her voice grew softer, tinged with the warmth of old memories.

"I can still picture that small sitting room, just enough space for a red three-seater sofa, a coffee table, and a fridge that doubled as a stand for our tiny TV. Those were simple times, but we were so happy."

Adaobi smiled, picturing the scene, as Chinelo seemingly brought the stories to life, painting pictures with her words.

"But then," Chinelo continued, her tone shifting as she delved into the next chapter of their lives, "everything changed. Osi's close childhood friend, Chief Igbokwe, was unexpectedly instated as a state governor after a shocking court ruling overturned the election results. None of us saw it coming, especially since the incumbent governor had already been inaugurated and was two months into his term. But Chief Igbokwe and his party were determined, and against all odds, they won."

Adaobi leaned in slightly, her curiosity piqued. Chinelo's stories always had a way of pulling her in, making her feel like she was right there, living through the twists and turns of life with her.

"The night Chief won the case," Chinelo continued, her voice taking on a conspiratorial tone, "he called Osi and a couple of other close friends for a meeting. He didn't give Osi an official title, but he became the Chief's right-hand man. The Chief would award him contracts directly, or he would help others secure them. Osi quickly became the point of reference for anyone who wanted a favor from the governor. You can't imagine the amount of money that started rolling in—just for setting up meetings or smoothing things over."

Chinelo's eyes sparkled as she recounted their sudden rise to wealth. "In just three months, we were rich beyond our wildest dreams. We bought a duplex on Victoria Island, paid for in cash, and filled our driveway with brand-new luxury cars—Mercedes, BMWs, Hondas, you name it. We were living like royalty, with housekeepers, cooks, valets, everything. You should have seen me, Nnem. I became one big madam overnight, living the high life."

Adaobi couldn't help but laugh, shaking her head in amazement.

"Wow, you guys were really living it up!"

"Yes oh!" Chinelo agreed, her eyes alight with the memory. "We were spending money like there was no tomorrow, traveling abroad on a whim. Imagine flying to London or America just for a weekend shopping spree. We threw lavish parties and lived like there was no end to the money."

She paused for a moment, her expression turning reflective as she continued, "On one of those trips, my cousin Onyi—you remember Onyi, right?"

"Yes, I met her at your place once," Adaobi replied, her interest piqued.

"That's the one," Chinelo confirmed. "Onyi suggested I apply for the American Visa Lottery, which was open at the time. I literally laughed in her face. It seemed like such a ridiculous idea at the time. Who would want to leave behind such a lavish lifestyle to come and struggle in America? We had the best of both worlds as it were."

Adaobi nodded, understanding the sentiment. "I can see why you thought that."

Chinelo chuckled, shaking her head at the memory. "I felt insulted, honestly. But Onyi wouldn't let up. She insisted I apply, arguing that if we won, it would save us the hassle of queuing up at the American embassy for visas—not that we ever queued, of course. We just sent our passports to the government house, and they took care of everything. She also suggested it could be useful for our kids if we wanted them to study in the USA someday. I countered all her arguments, but she wouldn't give up. So, to humor her, I finally agreed."

She laughed again, remembering the scene. "Onyi literally dragged me to a photo booth at the mall, made me take a passport picture, and then filled out the application online herself while I half-heartedly supplied the details. I forgot about it as soon as it was done. I wasn't planning on moving to the USA, not with the life we had back home."

Adaobi smiled, impressed by Onyi's persistence. "In retrospect, it was very prudent of her to insist you apply, especially since you won."

"Of course!" Chinelo agreed, her eyes twinkling. "But wait, you're jumping ahead. I haven't gotten to that part yet!"

"Sorry, I couldn't help it!" Adaobi laughed, eager to hear the rest of the story.

Chinelo's voice grew softer, almost reverent, as she relived those memories, her eyes reflecting the glow of the city lights outside. "So, after returning home, we slipped seamlessly back into our extravagant lifestyle, completely forgetting about the visa application. Did I mention that I had already quit my job by then? Osita insisted I do it. What I was earning in a month couldn't even cover the cost of one of the designer handbags I was carting around."

She paused, her voice dropping even lower, as if the weight of her confession required secrecy.

"Nnem, in those early days when I used to accompany Osi to the government house to visit Chief, I saw things that made me realize just how deep the rot goes in our leadership. I remember one visit so vividly—Chief had excused himself, only to return with a thick stack of dollar notes. Dollars, in a Nigerian State House!"

Adaobi's eyes widened, her disbelief almost palpable. "Dollars? In a Nigerian State House?"

"Yes, oh!" Chinelo confirmed, nodding emphatically. She mimicked the flicker of fingers beside her ears, the gesture that Chief had made as he handed out the wads of cash. "There were other guests there too, and he handed each of us a wad 'for kola nut.' I was so nervous, Nnem. My hands were trembling as I stuffed the money into my small handbag as fast as I could. I didn't know why Osi hadn't warned me to bring a bigger bag that day."

Adaobi leaned in closer, her curiosity piqued. "How much was it?"

Chinelo's eyes twinkled with the memory, a faint smile playing on the corners of her mouth. "A stack of 50 crisp, new 100-dollar notes. Each one of us in that room received a similar wad of dollar notes. Imagine—six of us, all walking away with stacks of dollars, just for 'kola nut.'"

Adaobi shook her head, marveling at the absurdity of it all. "That's incredible. You really did have a bite—a chunk, even—of that national cake."

Chinelo's smile faded, replaced by a frown of deep regret. "Yes, we did. But Nnem, everything comes at a price."

Adaobi sensed the gravity of her friend's words and pressed her gently. "So how did it all come to this?"

Chinelo sighed, the weight of her past evident in her voice. "Be patient, Nnem. The story is still unfolding."

"Okay, oh!" Adaobi said, her anticipation rising. She was eager to hear how Chinelo's life had taken such a dramatic turn.

Chinelo continued; her voice was steady tinged with nostalgia. "So, there we were, living the life, basking in our newfound riches. And as if we hadn't already been blessed with enough, I won the American visa lottery. Onyi called me out of the blue to say she had checked the results and that I had won. We reluctantly decided to follow through with the processing. And as if that wasn't enough, I discovered I was pregnant at the same time!"

Adaobi's face lit up, her excitement infectious. "Wow, pregnant too? It must have felt like you were on top of the world."

Chinelo nodded, her smile growing wider. "Life couldn't have been better. We were so happy. It didn't even matter that Osi was away most of the time, running errands for Chief. I had everything I needed—maids, parties to attend, trips abroad whenever I felt like it. But even as we reveled in our good fortune, the deposed governor was still contesting his termination. The case dragged on in court for over two and a half years, even as Chief remained in power."

Adaobi furrowed her brow, trying to piece together the timeline.

"But wasn't Chief's tenure almost over? They serve for four years, right?"

"Yes, four years," Chinelo confirmed, her tone shifting to one of bemusement. "There were only six months left of his tenure when the case was overturned again, this time ruling in favor of his opponent. But Nnem, do you think anyone cares about how much time is left? Just one month in the office is enough for someone to embezzle enough money to last a lifetime."

Adaobi shook her head in disbelief. "That's totally crazy."

As they approached Tollgates on the Triboro Bridge, Chinelo suddenly remembered something. "Nnem, please help pass my handbag from the back of the car. I forgot to get the money out for the toll beforehand."

Adaobi reached back, her hand brushing against the cool leather of the bag as she pulled it forward. She extracted a crisp five-dollar note, handing it to Chinelo with a knowing smile. "How much is it? I have some quarters if you need."

"Never mind, dear," Chinelo said, taking the note with a grateful nod. "This should cover it."

After handing the cash to the toll attendant and receiving the change, Chinelo drove through, the night lights of the city flickering past them as they headed for the Bronx exit.

"Now, please continue your gist. I'm dying to hear the rest." Adaobi urged impatiently.

Chinelo settled back into her seat while driving, her voice taking on a darker, more urgent tone. "So, the night before the court ruled to oust him from office, Chief frantically summoned Osita to the government house. It was as if he had a premonition about what was going to happen. Osi had confided in me that the Chief had already met with the presiding judge in secret. They had a private rendezvous on a jet just a few days earlier, where the Chief handed the judge about 30 million naira. The judge assured them the case was settled, that Chief would remain in power."

Adaobi gasped, her hand flying to her mouth in shock.

"They offered the judge that much money, and he still ruled against the Chief?"

"Yes, Nnem," Chinelo said, her voice tinged with bitterness. "It's a jungle out there. The highest bidder always wins. I bet the other camp offered the judge more money, which is why he ruled against the incumbent governor."

Adaobi shook her head, astonished at the betrayal. "I can't believe it. I'm so clueless about how those things work."

Chinelo sighed deeply; her gaze distant as she recalled the events.

"If I hadn't witnessed it firsthand, I wouldn't have believed it either. So, when Osita arrived at the government house that night, Chief entrusted him with about seven suitcases full of dollars, instructing him to take them to safety."

Adaobi's mouth dropped open in shock. "Seven suitcases? Full of dollars?"

"Yes, oh," Chinelo replied, her voice a hushed whisper. "Osita left the government house in an unmarked official car, with a chauffeur and an armed escort. They traveled all the way from the East back to Lagos that same night. By the time he got home, I was already asleep. I didn't even know he was back until I felt him slip into bed beside me."

Adaobi leaned forward, her eyes wide with anticipation. "Then what happened?"

Chinelo's voice softened; her tone almost tender as she recalled that moment. "He wrapped his arms around me and, half-asleep, I mumbled, "*Iba ta go, nno.* Are you back, welcome.' He urged me to go back to sleep, so that we'd talk in the morning. We cuddled up, and I dozed off, feeling safe in his embrace. But less than an hour later, we were jolted awake by frantic banging on our front door. The noise was so loud it shook the entire house, and I knew—deep in my bones—that everything was about to change."

"Who were they? Armed Robbers?" Adaobi tried to guess.

Chinelo's voice trembled as she recounted the nightmare that had unfolded that night. The memories were vivid, still haunting her despite the years that had passed.

"Yes, Nnem," she said, her voice barely above a whisper. "You guessed right—they were armed robbers. We're certain someone tipped them off. Maybe the government driver, or even the police officer who had accompanied Osita on the trip earlier. Or it could have been someone from the government house who knew about the money. But the real kicker was one black car—yeah, the one that Osi noticed following them from the start. He thought it was just another car at first, nothing unusual, but the way it trailed them—always at a distance, never close enough to be obvious but there, like a shadow."

Chinelo paused, letting the suspense linger in the air.

"The thing is, Osita wasn't the only one who felt it. The driver kept checking the mirrors more than usual, like he knew they weren't alone. And get this—the police officer who was with them earlier? Apparently, he was acting a little too friendly, you know? Like he knew something was about to go down."

Adaobi leaned forward, eyes wide. "You mean he was in on it?"

"Maybe. But Osita can't be sure. Could've been him, or the driver, or someone back at the government house. Whoever it was, they knew about the money. They knew the exact route, the exact time they were leaving. It wasn't some random attack."

Adaobi nodded thoughtfully, leaning back in her seat. "And the car?"

"That's the part that gets me," Chinelo continued. "Just as they were nearing home, it disappeared—vanished into thin air. Osita was scanning the road, expecting to see it, but no, nothing."

"If it was following them the whole time, why didn't they strike earlier?" Adaobi asked, her voice skeptical yet intrigued.

Chinelo's eyes gleamed with intensity. "That's exactly what Osita was wondering. He said it was too perfect—the timing, the way the car trailed them all the way but pulled off just before they got home. He thinks they were being watched the whole time, maybe even followed by more than just the car. They were waiting for something—maybe a signal, or maybe they didn't want to risk hitting them too close to the government house or on the streets, where they could have been seen."

Adaobi shuddered, wrapping her arms around herself. "Sounds like someone tipped them off. But who?"

"That's the mystery," Chinelo said, her voice dropping again. "It could've been anyone. The driver, the officer, someone back at the house. Whoever it was knew exactly what was going on, and they made sure that the black car followed them every step of the way. Osita said he's sure it wasn't just bad luck. Someone set them up."

She finished with a shake of her head, as if the weight of the story was still clinging to her.

Adaobi gasped, the horror of the situation sinking in. "Wow! Unbelievable!"

"Yes, oh," Chinelo continued, her body visibly shivering as the memories flooded back. "Osi whispered to me about the money as soon as the banging started. There was no doubt about what the robbers had come for. We were paralyzed with fear, clinging to each other under the bed and praying desperately that the intruders would leave if no one answered the door. Our gateman, Mallam, had strict orders never to open the gates to anyone unless we had given prior orders. We knew there was no way he would let them in, but the banging was so relentless, so loud, it etched through the walls, vibrating the very core of our home. We thought we were safe behind our sturdy gates…"

Chinelo paused, her breath catching as the terror of that night tightened its grip on her.

"After what felt like an eternity of that awful noise, everything went quiet. The silence was almost worse, Nnem. We thought—no, we hoped—that God had answered our prayers and that they had left. But that relief was cruelly short-lived. About thirty minutes later, they came back vigorously. This time, there was no mistaking their determination. We heard the unmistakable buzz of a drill, the crash of metal against metal. They were drilling through the gates, smashing through the wooden security panels behind the doors. The noise was deafening, like a storm tearing our world apart. They were coming in, Nnem, and there was nothing we could do to stop them."

Adaobi felt a shiver run down her spine. "That must have been terrifying. What did you do?"

"Terrifying doesn't even begin to describe it," Chinelo replied, her voice thick with emotion. "We were frantic, desperately searching for a place to hide. I tried to squeeze into my wardrobe, but the darkness, the suffocating air inside, made it impossible. I couldn't breathe. I tried to slide under the bed, but my pregnant belly—my precious baby—made it impossible. I begged Osi to hide, to let me try to reason with them, thinking they might take pity on me because of my condition. But he refused to leave my side. He was determined to protect me, even if it cost him his life. In the end, we had no choice but to stay together on the bed, holding each other like we were clinging to our last hope as the intruders stormed into our bedroom."

Her voice quivered; each word weighed with the terror of that night.

"They were like demons, Nnem—masks covering their faces, guns and machetes gleaming in the dim light. They were armed to the teeth, moving with the confidence of men who knew they had already won. I counted at least six or seven of them, but I was too scared to keep track. They started shouting, demanding money, and we didn't dare resist. We had already decided not to put up any fight that might get us killed. The fear was paralyzing."

Adaobi's heart pounded in her chest, the horror of the scene unfolding in her mind. "Did they take all the money?"

"Everything," Chinelo confirmed, her eyes dark with the memory.

"Not just the money, Nnem. They took everything—cash, computers, jewelry, watches. They stripped our home bare, like vultures picking a carcass clean. But that wasn't the worst of it."

Adaobi's eyes widened, her stomach twisting with dread. "What could be worse than that?"

Chinelo's voice grew colder, her face a mask of pain and anger.

"They violated us, Nnem. They dragged Osi from the bed, tied his hands and legs with rope, and beat him like he was nothing. They demanded to know where the money was, and when he tried to resist initially, they threatened to shoot him. I was lucky—if you can call it that—because I was heavily pregnant. They didn't rape me, but they came close. They groped me, Nnem, fondling me like I was some object, right in front of Osi, forcing him to watch. I could see the helplessness in his eyes, the pain of being unable to protect me."

Adaobi felt tears welling up in her eyes, her heart breaking for her friend. "Oh no…God, Chinelo, I'm so sorry."

Chinelo's expression hardened, the stoicism she had always carried now a shield against the pain. "They did worse to Nnedi, one of our house-helps. They raped her, Nnem. They tore her apart while the rest of our staff were beaten, humiliated. No one was spared. It was a nightmare—no, worse than a nightmare because we couldn't wake up from it. They tortured Osi for what felt like hours, battering him until he was barely conscious. And I—I was powerless, Nnem. All I could do was beg, plead, pray for it to end."

Adaobi was speechless, her mind struggling to understand the horror of it all. "None of your neighbors came to help. No one called the police?"

Chinelo let out a bitter laugh, devoid of any humor. "Nnem, you've been in America too long if you think that's how it works back home. No one would dare come out, not even our closest friends. They'd just be signing their own death warrant. And the police? Hah! Which police, Nnem? Who would they have called? Which number? And even if they did, do you think the police would come? Our good old police—half of them is in cahoots with criminals. The rest wouldn't risk their lives for the pennies they're paid."

"It's just so sad," Adaobi murmured, shaking her head, her eyes filled with tears.

Chinelo's voice grew even softer, the pain in her eyes deepening.

"The worst part was how it broke Osi. He was shattered—physically, mentally, emotionally. He kept lamenting how he had been overpowered in front of his wife, how he had failed to protect me. It crushed him, Nnem. It crushed his spirit."

Adaobi's heart ached for her friend, her own tears flowing freely now.

"But none of it was his fault, Chinelo. You both were victims."

Chinelo nodded, but the guilt in her eyes was unmistakable. "I know, but the guilt—it ate at him. After the robbers finally left, we were both rushed to the hospital—Osi for his injuries, and me…"

Her voice broke, the pain too much to bear. "I started bleeding, Nnem. Amid all that horror, I began to miscarry. We rushed to the hospital, but it was too late. I lost our baby girl. She was gone before we even had a chance to meet her, before she had a chance to live."

Tears streamed down Chinelo's face, her body trembling with the grief of her loss. Adaobi reached out and quickly pulled her friend into a brief side hug as they stopped at the red light. Words failed her.

They were both silent for a moment.

Adaobi's hand lingered on Chinelo's thigh, her touch warm and reassuring.

"Chinelo, I'm so sorry. If it's too much to talk about, we can stop right here," she offered gently, her voice a tender balm to the raw emotions that hung in the air. "Clara mentioned you had a miscarriage, but I never imagined it happened under such horrific circumstances. I can't begin to tell you how sorry I am."

Chinelo's breath hitched, her body shuddering with a wave of emotion she could barely hold. Adaobi quickly retrieved a tissue from the dashboard and handed it to her, watching as Chinelo dabbed at her eyes, trying to stem the tide of tears that had been waiting to break free.

Adaobi's voice softened even more as she repeated, "I'm so, so sorry."

Chinelo let out a sound that was part laugh, part sob, a bitter mix of emotions that mirrored the tumult in her heart.

"What are you apologizing for, Adaobi?" she asked, shaking her head as a faint smile tugged at the corners of her lips. "None of these was your fault. It was the will of God, or how else can I explain what happened that night? After we were discharged from the hospital, Osi and I knew we had to leave. As if by divine timing, our visa lottery documents came through, and it made the decision so much easier. If God doesn't work in mysterious ways, I don't know what to call it."

Adaobi nodded, her eyes full of understanding. "Everything happens for a reason," they say. But what about Chief? What did he say about his money?"

Chinelo sighed deeply, the weight of the past settling over her like a heavy cloak. "He was furious, of course, but there was nothing anyone could do. We never even found out how much money was in those suitcases or who took it. Chief couldn't openly declare it missing—not with the way it was acquired. He was devastated, especially since he was thrown out of the government house the very next day after the court ruled against him."

Adaobi's voice turned cold, a chill seeping into her words. "He must have had other stashes hidden away. Honestly, I don't feel much pity for him."

Chinelo gave a rueful smile, a spark of bitterness flickering in her eyes. "I know—it was never really his money to begin with. Afterward, the new governor hastily set up a government quasi-panel, but it was dissolved almost as quickly as it was formed. None of the corrupt officials have any interest in being scrutinized or, worse, setting a dangerous precedent that might lead to their own downfall. They're all too aware that the moment one of them is properly investigated, the rest will be next in line. It's nothing short of a sham—a kangaroo court, designed to give the appearance of action while protecting the guilty."

Chinelo paused, her expression turning wistful as she reflected on the past. "But even so, it was an absolutely dreadful time for everyone involved. For us, though, it became the breaking point, the final push we needed to make the decision to leave. We started liquidating everything, converting our assets into cash, selling off what we could, giving away items we couldn't, and entrusting the rest to family members, hoping they'd sell them and remit the money to us. It was a chaotic, heart-wrenching process, but at that point, we knew there was no turning back."

Adaobi looked at her with a raised eyebrow, her voice tinged with disbelief. "And they actually sold the items and sent you the money?"

Chinelo's laughter was hollow, echoing with the sound of betrayal.

"For where? I think we only received half the payment for one of our homes that we sold ourselves. My brothers-in-law even sold off our Victoria Island home barely five months after we left, the one we planned to rent out for a steady income."

Adaobi was aghast. "How could they do that without your consent?"

Chinelo's laughter turned sardonic, tinged with the bitterness of lessons learned. "Oh, Adaobi, you still have some of that naivety left in you, I see. To most of our relatives back home, once you live abroad, you're supposed to have everything, a cash cow that generates endless dollars. When Osi tried to reprimand his brothers for selling our home, they actually had the nerve to scold him!"

Adaobi shook her head in disbelief, her voice filled with shock. "I always thought it was a joke when people mentioned the things they go through with relatives back home."

"It's no joke, dear," Chinelo replied, her voice heavy with resignation. "There are so many misconceptions about life abroad. Sometimes I think our folks back home need a serious reality check. But you're lucky, Adaobi. You were born and bred here, only spending your teens back home. You're not as deeply tied to our culture as those of us who were born and raised there."

Adaobi nodded, her gaze thoughtful. "You could say that, but it's not that simple. I had my own struggles. When we returned to Nigeria, I had an identity crisis. I didn't know if I belonged to the American culture I was born into or the Nigerian culture my parents insisted on. It wasn't clear-cut at all."

Chinelo's eyes widened in surprise. "Ewo ooo, Adaobi, you see things we take for granted! I would never have guessed you faced any cultural identity crisis."

"It was real," Adaobi said, a bittersweet smile on her lips. "It felt like a subtle mental struggle, but it was very real at the time. I remember when we first arrived in the village, and my younger brother, Onisa ran for his life at the sight of a live cockerel. It was hilarious to everyone else but terrifying for him. He had never seen a real one before. I hadn't either, but I was older and could handle it better."

Chinelo burst into laughter, the sound rich and full, a welcome release from the tension of their earlier conversation. "Oh my God! Did you say Onisa actually ran from a mere cockerel?"

Adaobi joined in the laughter; the memory now more amusing than it had been at the time. "Yes, it sounds funny now, but Onisa had real nightmares for days afterward. I remember holding him at night, trying to calm him down. We shared a room back then, before we moved to our uncle's home in Lagos and had our own rooms. My point is most parents don't fully consider the cultural shock or struggles their kids might face when relocating back to their home country. They just expect you to adapt immediately."

Chinelo nodded, her laughter fading as she reflected on Adaobi's words.

"You're right. I must admit, I was ignorant of that. I never would have imagined you faced any cultural conflict. I thought you were privileged, with your accent and mannerisms. You were the one everyone wanted to be friends with."

"It wasn't all bad," Adaobi laughed. "There were perks, but it took real acclimatization."

The two friends fell into a brief, comfortable silence as Chinelo expertly exited I-287N, transitioning smoothly onto the local route that would take them through White Plains. They were coming from Brooklyn, and Chinelo was supposed to drop Adaobi off at a metro station in the Bronx, but their conversation had been so intense that she was unwittingly heading to White Plains, where Adaobi lived, before heading home to Scarsdale. The leafy streets and stately homes of the neighborhood, with their manicured lawns and quiet elegance, were a far cry from the bustling chaos they had once known in Lagos.

"So, what happened after you and Osi finally settled here?" Adaobi's queried, impatient to hear the rest of the story as she stole a quick glance at Chinelo, who was looking out the window, momentarily lost in thought.

Chinelo sighed, as if the memories she was about to share weighed heavily on her heart.

"Ah, my dear, where do I even begin? You know, we had previously traveled to the USA multiple times, so we thought we knew what to expect when we finally made up our minds to immigrate. We were determined to avoid the usual pitfalls that many immigrants face. We thought we had everything in our favor," she began, her voice steady but reflective.

Adaobi listened intently, her eyes flicking between the road and Chinelo, sensing there was much more to the story than just the logistics of moving.

"We were lucky, I suppose," Chinelo continued, her gaze fixed on the road ahead as they drove past the Westchester County Center. "We were scheduled to receive our green cards upon arrival, and after selling some of off our properties and withdrawing significant amounts from our bank accounts, we believed we had enough money to start a new life here in the USA—or so we thought."

A wry smile played on Chinelo's lips as she spoke. "Osi, being the man he is, was adamant that we wouldn't inconvenience ourselves or anyone else by squatting at someone's home. He insisted we move into our own place right from the start. We even asked Onyi to help us buy a house initially, but the short notice made that impossible. So, Osi suggested that Onyi help us rent an apartment instead."

Adaobi nodded, urging her to continue. "So, what happened when you got here?"

"When we landed at JFK, Onyi was waiting for us, ready to drive us straight to our new rented apartment," Chinelo recounted, a hint of nostalgia creeping into her voice. "I insisted on something moderately priced, even though Osi was still stuck on finding a place that matched our earlier social status. But Onyi, bless her, knew better than to listen to him. America, as you know, levels everyone, no matter what your background or status was back home."

"True," Adaobi agreed, her tone thoughtful, as Chinelo took a turn onto the quieter roads leading into White Plains.

"But things didn't go as smoothly as we'd planned," Chinelo continued, her voice tinged with a touch of regret. "We thought we'd settle in quickly—get our social security cards, work authorization, and secure suitable jobs, maybe even ones like our old jobs back home. But, as they say, man proposes, but God disposes."

Adaobi raised an eyebrow, curiosity piqued. "How long did it take before you found a job?"

Chinelo shook her head, a rueful smile on her lips. "Ages! Six months after we arrived, we were still searching for suitable jobs, naively hoping to find something that matched our qualifications from back home. Osi brushed aside Onyi's suggestions that we take any job we could find in the meantime. Our finances was dwindling fast. You know how it is when the money's only going out with nothing coming in."

"I can imagine," Adaobi murmured sympathetically.

"We kept ignoring Onyi's persistent warnings, even though she was practically begging us to take any job, just to tide us over. She repeatedly mentioned openings at places like Macy's, Lord & Taylor, Sears, or even fast-food joints like Mickey D's. But Osi was aggravated by those suggestions. He refused to take what he called 'dead-end jobs.'"

Chinelo's tone was a mix of frustration and sadness as she continued recalling those challenging times.

"Onyi never gave up on trying to help us avoid the usual pitfalls, she kept reminding us of her own journey because after studying Mass Communications back home, she had completely reinvented herself by going back to school and becoming a nurse here. She was always encouraging me, telling me I could do the same—that it wasn't too late to start fresh. She even offered to help me enroll in nursing school. But Osi wouldn't have it. He shut it down before I could even take the first step, refusing to let me pursue the idea at all."

Adaobi frowned, puzzled. "Why was he so stubborn?"

Chinelo sighed, her expression troubled. "Pride, maybe. Or perhaps it was the shock of realizing that the life we had back home didn't count for much here. We weren't paupers when we moved, far from it. But most of the places we applied to needed American certification, qualifications, or experience—things we didn't have. Osi was so adamant, so optimistic too that we'd break through somehow. But by the time we were down to about a tenth of the money we arrived with, I started sharing Onyi's anxiety."

Adaobi leaned in, captivated by the unfolding story. "So, what did you do?"

"I pleaded with Osi to let me find a job," Chinelo continued, her voice steadier and with an edge of resolve. "He finally conceded when it became clear that we'd be in even bigger trouble if all our money ran out. I applied for a Christmas job at Macy's a year after we arrived, and that was how I started working."

"Wow, Chinelo," Adaobi breathed, deeply moved by her friend's story. "That must have been incredibly tough."

"It was," Chinelo admitted, a wistful smile tugging at the corners of her mouth. "But that's life, isn't it? You plan, you prepare, but nothing can truly get you ready for the unexpected."

The car fell silent again as they entered a familiar neighborhood in White Plains, but this time it was a silence of mutual understanding and shared experiences.

"True," Adaobi agreed.

She knew there was more to the story and her heart ached for her friend. An unspoken pain lingered between them as they drove through the quiet, tree-lined streets of White Plains.

"Yes, Nnem, that's my story," Chinelo concluded, her voice tinged with exhaustion, as if the weight of her past had settled on her shoulders once more. The soft glow of the dashboard lights cast a somber hue over her face, highlighting the traces of pain etched into her expression.

"Wow, I feel your pain, Sis. It must have been rough," Adaobi said, her heart heavy with empathy. She stared out the window, watching the world outside blur into the twilight, the city lights flickering like distant stars against the encroaching darkness.

"Yes, it wasn't easy at all," Chinelo admitted, her voice barely above a whisper.

The memories of those challenging days clung to her like a shadow, never fully dissipating, wrapping her in a shroud of melancholy as they drove on.

"I would have expected Osi to be more understanding though, especially after all that you both had been through," Adaobi remarked, her tone growing more serious, more protective, like a lioness guarding her cub.

The silence between them was thick, almost suffocating, as they both grappled with the reality of the situation.

Chinelo sighed deeply, her grip tightening on the steering wheel as they approached Adaobi's apartment. The streetlights cast long, eerie shadows across the road, creating an almost surreal atmosphere, as if the world outside was reflecting the turmoil inside her heart.

"I know, my sister, which is why I strongly believe it's the work of the devil. The first time he laid his hands on me, it was completely uncalled for. I had prepared *egusi* soup for dinner—his favorite, or so I thought I knew—and he suddenly demanded *okra* soup instead. I gently asked if he could manage the *egusi* for the night, promising to make the *okra* the next day. He went silent, refused to touch the food, and the tension in the air was so thick you could cut it with a knife. When I started removing the dishes, he followed me into the kitchen. I turned back from the sink, and before I could even register what was happening, he slapped me across the face. The sting of the slap was nothing compared to the sting of betrayal. I could smell the alcohol on his breath."

"Just like that?" Adaobi asked, her voice laced with shock and disbelief. The image of Osi she once knew—a gentle, loving man—was now a shattered illusion, replaced by this unsettling new reality.

"Yes, just like that," Chinelo confirmed, her voice quivering as she relived that moment. "He was apologetic at once, but in the same breath, he accused me of arguing with him. Between you and me, there was no argument. I had simply asked if I could prepare the *okra* soup the next day. I was too tired to start making another fresh pot of soup after a long day at work."

"There's no justifiable reason for any man to lay his hands on a woman. None. He had no right to hit you," Adaobi insisted, her voice thick with anger, her heart pounding in her chest. The thought of her friend enduring such pain ignited a fierce protective instinct within her.

"I know," Chinelo replied softly, as they turned onto the familiar streets leading to Adaobi's apartment. The buildings loomed over them, silent witnesses to the emotional storm brewing inside the car.

"I just pray that this is a rough patch that will pass for us. The Osi I knew wouldn't hurt a fly, much less me."

"Have you suggested that he seek proper help? Is he drinking too much or doing any drugs?" Adaobi asked, her concern deepening as she searched Chinelo's face for answers. The thought of Osi's behavior being influenced by something more sinister gnawed at her.

"No, not at all," Chinelo denied vehemently, defending Osi with a fierceness born of love and loyalty. "He isn't that kind of person. He doesn't smoke, and he only drinks occasional beer. He would never touch drugs. I can vouch for him on that with my life."

"Okay, but what about getting professional care?" Adaobi suggested cautiously, knowing this might be a sensitive subject. Her words hung in the air, heavy with the implications of what she was suggesting.

"You mean, like seeing a shrink?" Chinelo asked, her tone a mix of skepticism and curiosity as she glanced at Adaobi, the headlights of an oncoming car briefly illuminating her doubtful expression.

"Yes, a psychiatrist, psychotherapist, counselor, or even your priest—anyone who could help him explore what's really going on," Adaobi explained, her tone firm but gentle, as they passed through the last stretch of road before reaching their destination. Even as she made the suggestion, Adaobi knew that the notion of pursuing mental health care was still so foreign, especially within their culture. She knew how her people viewed therapy—as a sign of weakness, something only for the "troubled" or "crazy." But Osi's recent struggles were undeniable, and Adaobi knew deep down that this was beyond what a simple conversation with friends or family could resolve. Mental health care wasn't a weakness; it was necessary for healing, and Osi needed healing more than ever.

"That's for oyibo—white folks, you know," Chinelo countered, her voice tinged with cultural hesitation, the weight of tradition holding her back. The stigma surrounding mental health in their community loomed large, an invisible barrier that seemed almost impossible to break.

"That's a big misconception, my dear. From what you've told me, Osi needs help, and I mean professional help. He might be depressed," Adaobi suggested, her voice tinged with worry. The thought of her friend suffering in silence tore at her heart, and she knew she had to convince Chinelo to take action.

"I know something is wrong, even if I can't exactly put my finger on it. But I'm praying this is just a passing phase. I genuinely believe he'll be fine. We'll be fine," Chinelo repeated, her voice wavering slightly as if she was trying to convince herself more than anyone else.

The uncertainty in her words lingered in the air, mingling with the tension as they finally pulled up to Adaobi's apartment, the night closing in around them like a heavy curtain.

"I wish I could share your optimism, but I'll pray for you too. Please, my dear, think seriously about encouraging him to seek professional help," Adaobi urged again, her voice filled with deep concern, the weight of her words hanging in the air like a plea. The urgency in her tone carried a desperate hope that Chinelo would heed her advice, a hope rooted in the strength of their friendship.

"I'll try but I doubt Osi will ever agree to it. I'll see what I can do to convince him," Chinelo promised, though her voice was heavy with uncertainty. As the words left her lips, they echoed in the quiet of the car, mingling with the low hum of the engine. A small part of her clung to the possibility of change, but the road ahead seemed fraught with challenges.

As they neared Adaobi's apartment, the familiar streets of White Plains, lined with towering trees and stately homes, began to unfold before them. The evening light cast long shadows across the pavement, painting the scene with a quiet serenity that contrasted with the turmoil in Chinelo's heart.

She slowed the car down and suggested, "See, we got carried away and I was just driving straight to your home rather than the nearest Metro in the Bronx." A small smile played on her lips, a rare moment of lightness amid the heavy conversation.

"I know, we were both too engrossed in the conversation but thanks, Chi, it's really nice of you to drive me home," Adaobi replied, her tone softening as she glanced at her friend. "You can take the next exit, and I'll guide you to our home."

"Okay," Chinelo responded, her grip on the steering wheel relaxing as she followed the exit. The tension in the car began to ease as they approached the familiar route, memories of their old friendship bubbling to the surface.

"I can't believe this is the first proper chat we've had since we reconnected," Adaobi remarked, trying to lighten the mood. The nostalgia in her voice was unmistakable, a gentle reminder of the bond they once shared. The familiar roads seemed to echo with the laughter and stories of their younger days.

"I know, that's the white man's land for you," Chinelo joked, a soft laugh escaping her lips. "It's all work, bills, and more bills to pay. Our folks back home are having more fun, yet they don't seem to realize their luck." Her words carried a hint of longing for the simpler days back in Nigeria, where life moved at a different pace.

"True," Adaobi agreed, her spirits lifting slightly as they passed by homes that seemed to glow with warmth and comfort.

The streetlights began to flicker on, casting a golden hue over the road.

"Should I make a left or right at the traffic light?" Chinelo asked, the familiarity of the streets bringing a sense of calm.

"Left, then the second right, and drive towards the end of St. Nicholas Road. Take the last left," Adaobi instructed, her voice steady and clear.

"I remember this route now," Chinelo said as she made the right turn, the car gliding smoothly down the road. "I'll make the next left, and then your house is the second on the right."

"Yes, that's right. You must have an incredibly good memory," Adaobi remarked, impressed by Chinelo's ability to recall the route with such precision. "If I recall correctly, you've only been to our home once, when you dropped Clara off."

"Yes, I'm actually good at remembering roads and routes," Chinelo responded modestly, a hint of pride in her voice.

"Anyway, we should really try to meet up more often and maybe plan that holiday together, like we discussed with Clara and Ifeyinwa. Ikunnu can join us from Nigeria or if she happens to be around in the USA as well," Adaobi suggested, her tone filled with excitement at the prospect of rekindling their friendship through shared adventures.

"Yes, we should. That sounds like a great plan," Chinelo agreed, her voice filled with a renewed sense of hope. The idea of a getaway with her friends was like a ray of sunshine piercing through the clouds of her current worries.

"You even avoided Ms. Davis's driveway, or was that just coincidental?" Adaobi asked, raising an eyebrow as Chinelo pulled up two doors away from her apartment building.

"Purely coincidental," Chinelo assured her with a grin. "But now that you bring it up, I sure recall you mentioning your rather mischievous neighbor in the past. Is she still being nosey?"

"Haha, yes! Our neighbor, Ms. Davis, she's definitely still as nosey as ever! You wouldn't believe it, but she seems to have a radar for every small thing happening in the neighborhood. The other day, I got a knock on the door just minutes after bringing in my groceries because I had parked a little too close to her driveway for her liking. She gave me the usual rundown about how *"proper parking"* ensures everyone's safety. It's a routine at this point!"

Adaobi laughed before continuing, "She's also the self-appointed "lawn inspector." If the grass gets just a little bit too long, she'll make a casual comment, like, "Looks like someone's been too busy to mow the lawn." And of course, trash day is her favorite. Heavens forbid you leave your bins out past Wednesday morning; she'll have them neatly placed by your garage before you even realize it! Honestly, though, she means well. I think she just likes things a little too... *organized*, you know? Keeps the neighborhood in tip-top shape, even if it drives everyone a little mad!"

The tension that had gripped them earlier seemed to dissipate, replaced by the warmth of shared humor and understanding.

"Thanks again for the ride. It was fun catching up. Please take care of yourself and remember, for both your sake and Osi's, to encourage him to seek the right help," Adaobi urged one last time, her voice filled with sincerity.

"I'll try," Chinelo promised, her voice soft yet resolute. There was a quiet strength in her words, a hint of unspoken determination that made her resolve even more palpable.

"Bye, dear," Adaobi bade warmly, her heart full of concern for her friend. The streetlight cast a soft glow over her as she stepped out of the car, the night air cool against her skin.

"Bye, Nnem, it was a joy riding with you," Chinelo repeated before they hugged goodbye.

As Chinelo drove away, the quiet hum of the engine filled the silence as she headed towards her home in Scarsdale. The road ahead was dark, but the lights in the distance offered a glimmer of hope, guiding her through the night.

IFEYINWA

"I should be on my way now, Clara dear, I guess I am the last one to leave." Ifeyinwa said as she rose to her feet, the weight of responsibility tugging at her. "I still have to pick the kids from school."

She began packing up her bags, moving with the practiced efficiency of a mother who always had a dozen things to juggle at once. The soft rustle of her movements filled the room, a gentle contrast to the lively chatter that had filled their gathering moments before.

Ikunnu had already departed a few hours ago to her hotel in Manhattan.

"Thank you once again, you all really made my day," Clara exclaimed, her voice radiating with heartfelt gratitude. The warmth in her eyes was unmistakable, sparkling with the depth of her appreciation. "I know how hectic our lives can be, so I'm truly touched that each of you took the time to visit me today. It means more to me than I can say."

"What are friends for?" Ifeyinwa countered with a playful smile, her tone light but sincere. She didn't expect an answer, it was a rhetorical question, after all. "Anyway, just take care of yourself and like we've all reminded you, get some proper rest now that you can." She wagged her forefinger at Clara, emphasizing her point with a mock sternness that only close friends could share.

"I'll try," Clara promised, though there was a glint of determination in her eyes. "I feel so much stronger and recovered already, but I still have two weeks before I return to work."

"You should relish this free time while recuperating, and don't you dare return to work before time," Ifeyinwa repeated, her voice firm. "There's always someone else to do the job when you aren't there. Take care of yourself for a change."

"I hear you," Clara replied, a small chuckle escaping her as she started toward the kitchen. "You mustn't forget to take the crayfish and okra that I promised you." She returned moments later with three sizeable zip-lock packs of crayfish, okra, and bitter leaf, handing them over to Ifeyinwa with a smile.

"Thanks, dear. They will surely come in handy," Ifeyinwa said gratefully, her eyes lighting up at the sight of the familiar ingredients.

"And thanks for the drinks and biscuits you already gave me for the kids. Oh dear, you added bitter leaf too. You had some to spare?" Ifeyinwa asked, noticing the extra pack of bitter leaf that Clara had slipped in along with the okra and crayfish.

"*Dalu so*," she continued, expressing her gratitude in Igbo. "I haven't made okra or bitter leaf soup in a long while. I still haven't had the chance to locate an African shop to buy food products since we moved to the City of Elizabeth."

"Don't remind me of those pricey African shops," Clara joked, rolling her eyes dramatically. "I haven't been to one in ages myself. We're lucky to have guests visiting from home frequently. They usually bring us foodstuffs and other condiments, so I haven't had to bother buying them from the stores here."

"Lucky you," Ifeyinwa said with a small sigh. "We rarely have any visitors. The few we get want to take from us instead! Thanks once again."

As they walked to Ifeyinwa's car, the late afternoon sun bathed the neighborhood in a warm, amber light, casting a gentle glow that softened the edges of everything it touched.

Clara's expression grew more serious as she asked, "Are you still hoping to sit for your medical licensing exams?"

"I still hope to, my dear," Ifeyinwa confessed, her voice tinged with uncertainty. "But sincerely, I fear that the more years I'm out of proper medical practice, the more difficult it will be to convince anyone to give me a job in the future."

"I wouldn't worry about that now," Clara advised gently, her tone filled with reassurance. "You'll cross that bridge when you reach it. The major thing to do first is sit for the exams."

"I hope that I find the time," Ifeyinwa replied, a note of frustration creeping into her voice. "There's too much on my plate to contend with presently. You know our situation, and I must look after the kids too and work. I don't know how I'll cope if I must combine studies with all of that. Those exams are tough, you know."

"I understand your difficulties," Clara concurred, nodding sympathetically. "But I don't want you to lose sight of your dream. You didn't endure rigorous medical school training back home to come to America and settle for being a home health attendant." Clara's voice grew more intense, her words driven by the strength of her belief in her friend. "Not that there's anything wrong with the HHA job, but you might as well use your medical degree than let it go to waste."

"It's not that you said it, dear, it bothers me too," Ifeyinwa admitted, her eyes betraying the deep concern she felt. "I really have to start making serious preparations about sitting for the exams."

"You must," Clara insisted, her tone firm. "A few years down the line, you'll regret why you never gave it a shot."

"True talk, my dear," Ifeyinwa agreed, a note of resolve entering her voice. She reached out to hug Clara, the embrace filled with warmth and gratitude. "Thank God for you," she prayed softly. "You always try to keep us all in focus."

"We are all each other's keepers," Clara replied modestly, brushing off the praise with a gentle smile. "Otherwise, it wouldn't make sense that we're all here together."

"You're still nothing short of a gem," Ifeyinwa said, her voice thick with emotion.

"C'mon, stop," Clara urged, feeling a bit self-conscious under the weight of such heartfelt words. "After you sit for and pass your medical exams, get a job, and invite us to visit your new plush mansion, then you can heap accolades on me."

"You know I will," Ifeyinwa promised, her smile broadening at the thought of the future Clara painted.

"And I know you can do it, and that's the beauty of America," Clara continued, her voice filled with conviction. "If one is really hardworking, dedicated, and perseveres, then all their dreams are achievable."

"Yes, the almighty American dream," Ifeyinwa retorted, though there was a hint of doubt in her tone.

"Lose the cynicism, Ifeyi dear," Clara chastised with a laugh, playfully patting her on the shoulder. "It doesn't become you. I know you're quite capable of achieving any dream. It's only a matter of time plus hard work, dedication, and tenacity, none of which you're lacking!"

"So says my wonderful friend, and I have to believe it," Ifeyinwa responded, her spirits lifting under Clara's encouragement.

"You better; you don't have any other choice," Clara warned half-seriously, her eyes sparkling with humor.

They laughed, the sound of their shared joy echoing down the quiet street as they chatted some more before hugging once again and parting ways.

Ifeyinwa climbed into her car, her heart lighter than it had been in weeks. As she drove back to The City of Elizabeth, New Jersey, where she lived, she slid in her religious cassettes, the familiar melodies of praise worship songs filling the car. She sang along, her voice blending with the music as she made the hour-long trip, arriving just in time to pick up her kids from school.

Their excited chatter filled the car as they bundled in, and as she drove them home, Ifeyinwa felt a renewed sense of purpose, she would find a way to make her dreams a reality.

"Fasten your seatbelt, Ofor," Ifeyinwa gently urged her 6-year-old son, her tone a mix of motherly love and the exhaustion that comes with juggling so many responsibilities. She leaned over to buckle her 4-year-old daughter, Uju, into her car seat, her hands moving with practiced ease despite the fatigue in her bones.

"There are some biscuits and soda in the back if you want some. Aunty Clara bought them for you. Don't forget to thank her the next time she calls, okay?"

"Yes, Mummy," the children chorused, their voices bright and innocent, oblivious to the weariness behind their mother's smile.

They had only been on the road for a few minutes when Ofor piped up from the backseat, "Mummy, mummy, can we get Mickey Dee?" His voice was filled with the boundless enthusiasm that only children possess, the kind that made every small desire seem like the most important thing in the world.

"Yes, yes, mummy! Can we get some?" Uju echoed, her eyes wide with anticipation as she latched onto her older brother's request.

Ifeyinwa's heart tightened. She wanted to say yes, to pull into the nearest McDonald's and let them indulge in the treat they so clearly craved. But her mind was already calculating the cost, not just in dollars but in the sacrifices, she'd have to make elsewhere. "No, Ofor and Uju, Mummy is going to make some rice when we get home. I made a delicious chicken stew yesterday," she suggested, her voice light and encouraging, trying to steer them away from their fast-food fantasy.

"Who likes chicken?" she asked, throwing in a playful tone to distract them, hoping their youthful excitement would shift gears.

"Me!" Uju responded with delight, her tiny hand shooting into the air as if she were in a classroom, eager to be the first to answer.

But Ofor was not so easily swayed. "But mummy, you promised to get us burgers," he protested, his voice carrying the weight of a broken promise, real or imagined.

"Did I promise to get some today?" Ifeyinwa returned, her tone brisk, but with a hint of regret for having to deny them something so simple.

Ofor hesitated, then reluctantly admitted, "No."

"So, we'll get McDonald's another day. Today, Mummy says we're eating rice," she repeated firmly, the finality in her voice leaving no room for negotiation.

There was a moment of silence, the kind that always follows when a child contemplates whether to keep pushing or to concede.

Finally, Ofor relented, though not without a last-ditch effort.

"Okay, Mummy. But can I have two pieces of chicken?" His voice was softer now, almost pleading, as if the extra piece of chicken could somehow compensate for the loss of a Happy Meal.

Ifeyinwa's heart ached with guilt. "Of course, you can," she agreed readily, her earlier firmness melting into affection.

As she glanced at them through the rearview mirror, a pang of sorrow hit her. It wasn't just about the burgers—they were too young to understand the financial strain she was under. They couldn't grasp the silent battle she fought every day to provide for them, to keep their lives as normal and happy as possible.

She wanted to give them everything they asked for, but the reality of their situation made that impossible. In retrospect, she rationalized that it was better this way—better that they grew up appreciating home-cooked meals over fast food, that they learned the value of what they had rather than what they lacked. But the knowledge did little to soothe the guilt that gnawed at her.

As they continued driving, the mood in the car seemed to lighten until Ofor's small voice broke the fragile peace. "Is Daddy coming tomorrow?" he asked, his tone casual, as if the question were as simple as asking about the weather.

"Is Daddy coming tomorrow?" Uju echoed, her innocent voice full of hope.

Ifeyinwa's grip tightened on the steering wheel. "I hope so, or maybe the day after," she said, keeping her voice steady despite the turmoil that brewed within her. She hated these moments, those innocent questions that forced her to confront the lies she had to tell.

"Why does Daddy have to live away from us?" Uju asked, her curiosity as pure as her young heart.

Before Ifeyinwa could formulate an answer, Ofor jumped in.

"Dumb! He works away from home," he said with the impatience of an older sibling who's heard the question too many times.

Ifeyinwa's heart clenched. "Ofor, I've warned you about name-calling," she chided, her voice stern but laced with a deep sadness. "You don't refer to your sister—or anyone else—by anything other than their proper names."

Ofor ducked his head, his earlier bravado deflating. "I'm sorry, Mummy. But Uju keeps asking the same questions all the time."

"But I want Daddy to be at home with us every day," Uju whined, her voice tinged with the kind of longing that only a child could express so openly.

"He will be, once he gets a job closer to home," Ofor responded, his tone more soothing now, as if he understood, on some level, that his sister needed comfort more than answers.

"Okay," Uju said, her small voice accepting this explanation, her attention quickly returning to the toy in her lap.

Ifeyinwa's breath hitched as she realized how close she'd come to another painful conversation. She and her husband, Christopher, had agreed long ago to shield the truth from their children for as long as possible. How could she explain to them that their father was living a double life, that they were divorced on paper, and that he had remarried a woman named Latoya for immigration purposes? How could she make them understand that while their father lived with another woman, he still tried to maintain the facade of a family with them?

It was a web of lies that she herself had trouble navigating, let alone explaining to her young children. So, she stuck to the narrative they'd created: Daddy was working far from home, but one day, he'd be back for good. She prayed that by the time they were old enough to see through the lies, their situation would have changed for the better, and the truth wouldn't hurt as much.

For now, she was just grateful that Ofor had unknowingly spared her the agony of further deception. She focused on the road ahead, her thoughts a mix of determination and desperation, hoping that one day, the truth would be kinder to them all.

Still, Ifeyinwa's current situation weighed on her more heavily than she would ever admit out loud. The tangled web of her life had grown more complicated, more fraught with uncertainty, than she had ever imagined possible. Her children, blissfully unaware of the truth, carried on with their innocent questions and simple joys, while she struggled to keep the cracks in her world from showing.

Her husband—no, her ex-husband—no, her husband. Even in her thoughts, Ifeyinwa was confused about how to refer to him.

Christopher was still hers, wasn't he? Yet he lived with Latoya now, and it seemed that Latoya's words, Latoya's opinions, held more sway over him than hers ever could. Christopher swore that he and Latoya didn't share a bed, and Ifeyinwa chose to believe him. She had to. Believing in him was the only way she could hold onto her sanity, the only way to keep her world from collapsing entirely.

But doubt was a cruel companion. It gnawed at the edges of her mind, whispering dark possibilities whenever she allowed herself a moment of reflection.

What was really going on between Christopher and Latoya? They lived in the same house but in separate rooms. Was that even possible? And why was she, his true wife, not allowed to see for herself? Christopher had been adamant: Latoya had threatened to expose their marriage as a scam if Ifeyinwa ever set foot in their home. She had promised to call immigration and have them all deported—Christopher, Ifeyinwa, and even the children.

The fear of losing everything, of being sent back to Nigeria with nothing to show for their years of struggle, kept Ifeyinwa at bay. She couldn't afford to take that risk.

So, she endured. She waited. Until their immigration status was resolved, she couldn't live with her real husband or even visit his new home. She had to be content with the occasional weekends when Latoya allowed him to visit his family.

This was far from the American dream they had envisioned, Ifeyinwa thought bitterly. This life—this fractured existence—was a far cry from the grand plans they had made together.

In retrospect, Ifeyinwa could hardly believe how foolish she had been to think it would all go according to plan. Nothing in her life, nothing in her marriage to Christopher, had ever gone exactly as planned. The thought brought a small, rueful smile to her lips. How naive they had been; to think they could control the chaos of life with mere plans.

As she sat there, driving her children home, her thoughts heavy with both regret and longing, she couldn't help but wonder where it had all gone wrong. How had the dream turned into this nightmare of half-truths and sacrifices? And yet, despite everything, she held on. She had to. For her children, for herself, for the hope that one day, their plans might still come true.

Ifeyinwa's thoughts drifted back to her childhood, to those days filled with the simplicity and innocence that only youth can bring. Life had seemed so straightforward then, so free of the burdens that now weighed her down.

Her parents were modest people, unassuming and content with their lot in life. Her father, a diligent trader, and her mother, a devoted housewife, created a world for her that was safe and predictable.

Growing up in Aba, a vibrant and industrious city nestled in southeastern Nigeria, Ifeyinwa, while immersed in a world brimming with energy and promise, knew nothing of the complexities that would later define her life. The city's blend of modernity and tradition, its vibrant markets, and its rich cultural heritage created a backdrop that was both formative and foundational for her.

The days were filled with routine—a rhythm of meals, minor chores, extra lessons after school, and endless play with friends.

Their neighborhood was lively, teeming with traders and businessmen, most of whom were indigenes like her family. Her father, a man of little formal education, had worked his way up from years of apprenticeship to become a successful seller of building blocks. Her mother, who had completed elementary school before settling into her role as a housewife, supported him in every way she could.

Ifeyinwa, their firstborn of five children, was the apple of their eyes, yet she always knew her place.

Her father had plans for all his children, but the weight of his expectations fell most heavily on her brother, Achonam, the third child and only son. The girls, including Ifeyinwa, were to receive a basic education—enough to get by in life. But for Achonam, her father dreamed bigger. He wanted him to attend university, to rise above the status of a mere trader and make something more of himself.

As for his daughters, higher education was discouraged, almost frowned upon. Her father had no patience for what he called "I.T.K. women"—the "I too know" women, those overly educated women who, in his eyes, challenged the natural order by aspiring to be equals with men. He echoed the sentiments of Fela, his favorite artist, who sang about women who wanted to sit at the table before everyone else, who dared to take a piece of meat before the men.

Her father's disdain for untraditional women was no secret. He believed firmly in the roles assigned by tradition, where a woman's place was in the home, raising children, not in the world of men. To go against his wishes was unthinkable. He was a good man, strict but fair, and his word was law. He rarely had to raise his voice; a single stern look was enough to keep his children in line.

And so, the plan was always clear—Ifeyinwa was to get a basic education, complete primary school, perhaps even secondary school if her father allowed it. But that was as far as her ambitions were supposed to go.

Looking back now, Ifeyinwa could see how her life had been shaped by those early expectations, by the limits that had been set for her before she even understood what dreams were. There was no room for questioning, no space for rebellion. Her father's plans were her plans, his dreams, her boundaries.

As soon as Ifeyinwa started school, it became clear that she was no ordinary student. Her quick grasp of lessons and unwavering dedication made her stand out, catching the attention of her teachers. Her parents soon started envisioning a more modest future for her, perhaps attending a teacher training college and becoming a schoolteacher before settling down into marriage.

When Ifeyinwa completed her secondary education with an impressive seven straight A's and two distinctions, her school principal and teachers insisted that her parents reconsider their initial plans. They argued that it would be a disservice to her natural intelligence if she weren't allowed to pursue higher education.

During a parent-teacher meeting, the principal spoke directly to Ifeyinwa's father. "Mr. Okafor, your daughter is exceptional. She has the potential to excel far beyond what we see here. It would be a great loss if her education were cut short."

Her father shifted uncomfortably in his chair, hesitant. "I understand what you're saying, but... we have other plans for Ifeyinwa. She is to marry soon and start a family."

The principal shook her head gently, her voice resolute but respectful.

"With all due respect, sir, Ifeyinwa can still have a family, but she can also make a name for herself—perhaps as a doctor or an engineer. Her mind is sharp, her ambition endless. It would be a disservice not to give her that chance."

Her mother, who had been silent up until then, spoke softly. "But what if we push her too far? What if it's too much for her?"

Ifeyinwa, seated quietly at the table, suddenly found her voice.

"Mama, I want this. I know I can do it."

Her mother turned to her, worry in her eyes. "Your father and I only want what's best for you."

"I know," Ifeyinwa replied gently. "But imagine—imagine me as a doctor. Think of what I could do, how I could help people, how proud you would be."

Her father frowned, still reluctant. "It's a lot of money, and time... We had hoped for a simpler path for you."

The room was silent for a moment, but her principal broke it with conviction. "She is worth the investment, Mr. Okafor. Your daughter can accomplish great things."

It took time, and many more conversations, but eventually, her parents came around.

One evening, her father finally spoke with a sigh, "Alright, Ifeyinwa. If this is truly what you want, we will support you. But remember, this is no small dream you are chasing."

Her mother smiled faintly, placing a hand on Ifeyinwa's. "We will dream bigger for you, my child."

With those words, they allowed themselves to imagine her not as the young bride they had planned, but as a doctor, lawyer, or engineer. The possibilities were endless, and for the first time, they began to see their daughter's future as something extraordinary.

Ifeyinwa, however, had not initially planned for university, so she enrolled in high school while waiting to sit for the Joint Admissions and Matriculation Board (JAMB) exams, a requirement for university entry in Nigeria.

When the results came out, Ifeyinwa had predictably excelled, earning scores that secured her a place to study Medicine at the University of Port Harcourt.

Her matriculation day was a monumental event. Ifeyinwa became the first female in her family—as well as the first aspiring female doctor in her family —to attend university.

Her parents were bursting with pride as they stood in the crowded hall, surrounded by other proud parents and their children, witnessing their daughter take her first steps toward a future none of them had dared to dream of before.

Ifeyinwa, however, remained humble and focused. She didn't let the excitement get to her head. Instead, she sought solace in spirituality, joining the Scripture Union (SU) at the university, an organization known for its dedication to Christian values.

One of the girls from her neighborhood often joked that SU girls were left unbothered on campus because no one cared much about their simple attire or reserved demeanor. Ifeyinwa found comfort in this. She didn't want the pressures of popularity or the distractions that came with it. For her, the focus was on her studies and her faith. The SU provided a shield, a sanctuary where she could immerse herself in both.

Over the next six years, she dedicated herself to her medical studies, the scriptures, and spreading the word of God. Her modest wardrobe and simple lifestyle kept her away from the social rivalries that were common on campus. While other students frequented expensive restaurants and wore the latest fashion trends, Ifeyinwa found contentment in the school canteen and her small circle of "born-again sisters."

It was also during this pivotal period in the university that she met a group of other friends who would become integral to her life. Clara, who became her roommate in her second year, was a significant influence. Their bond was instant and profound, and they maintained a strong connection throughout their lives. Clara's vibrant personality and unwavering support has also become a cornerstone for Ifeyinwa, especially during her current trying time.

In addition to Clara, Ifeyinwa also met Chinelo, a classmate of Clara's, and their friendship blossomed. Through Clara, Ifeyinwa was introduced to Adaobi, whose presence added another layer of camaraderie to her university experience. Their shared moments and mutual support helped create a network of friends that would sustain her through various stages of her life.

Ikunnu, Clara's cousin, was yet another important link in this intricate web of friendships. Though Ikunnu still lived in Nigeria, her occasional visits brought a fresh perspective and enriched their circle with her experiences from afar.

During one of the SU Bible study meetings while they were still in UniPort, Ifeyinwa had truly connected with Christopher. Though they had known each other through prayer meetings and mutual friends, it wasn't until her final year that their paths aligned in a significant way.

They were gathered for prayers one faithful day and the room was filled with a palpable sense of peace during a quiet moment of reflection. Christopher's voice had suddenly rung out, breaking the silence. His eyes were closed, and his face was lit with conviction. "The Holy Spirit has spoken to me," he said, his voice steady and sure. "Ifeyinwa and I are destined to marry."

The room fell silent. Ifeyinwa's heart skipped a beat as she felt the weight of his words settle over her. She glanced at him, her mind racing. Yet, in her heart, there was no confusion, no hesitation. It felt right.

Later, when they spoke alone, Christopher reiterated his words from earlier. "I know this might seem sudden, but I'm certain of what I heard. We are meant to be together, Ifeyinwa."

She smiled softly, her answer already clear in her mind. "I feel it too," she replied. "It's not just about what was said today. I've been thinking about it for a while... and the fact that we're from the same area makes it all the more right. I trust you, Christopher."

Christopher took her hand, relief and joy crossing his face. "I will honor you. I promise you that."

For Ifeyinwa, it wasn't a difficult decision. Marrying Christopher felt like the natural course of things, as though every step of her life had led her to this moment. With his declaration and their shared faith, it seemed like everything had fallen perfectly into place.

Her parents, who were lately more focused on her education, were already beginning to worry about her future. Each time she returned home for holidays without a suitor, their concern grew. They feared that with all her education, she might struggle to find a husband.

So, when Ifeyinwa returned home that Christmas with the news that she would wed Christopher, their relief was palpable.

Her family quickly investigated Christopher's background and were delighted to find that he hailed from her maternal hometown, Bende. Their approval was swift, and soon the plans for their wedding were set in motion.

Ifeyinwa's mind wandered back to the early days of their journey, a time now cloaked in nostalgia and bittersweet memories. It was almost seven years ago to the day when she and Christopher had touched down at Newark Airport, stepping into a world far beyond their wildest imaginings.

Back then, the thought of living abroad was a distant, almost fanciful dream. Neither Ifeyinwa nor Christopher had ever truly imagined themselves leaving their familiar world behind.

Their wedding, a modest but meaningful ceremony, had been a simple affair after their graduation and NYSC service year. Ifeyinwa continued diligently with her internship at a local hospital, while Christopher ventured to Lagos, where his uncle's promise of future employment seemed like a beacon of hope. His uncle's connections were supposed to open doors—Christopher with a ministry job and Ifeyinwa with a coveted position at Lagos University Teaching Hospital (LUTH).

Yet, reality had a way of muddling dreams.

In Lagos, Christopher found himself tangled in a web of missed opportunities. He worked at his uncle's freight and forwarding company; a job far removed from his aspirations.

Daily, he passed by the American embassy, observing the seemingly endless queues of hopefuls waiting for visas. Their persistent presence fascinated him. He wondered why, despite the seasons shifting and time marching on, the lines never seemed to shorten. The thought of joining them never crossed his mind.

One serendipitous day, as Christopher made his way to the bus stop, he ran into Sam, a childhood friend who was on his way to an interview at the American embassy.

"Hey Chris, long time no see!" Sam called out, waving energetically.

"Sam! What are you doing here?" Christopher asked, surprised to see his old friend.

"I've got an interview at the embassy," Sam said, grinning. "I'm applying for a visa. You should come with me. You never know, you might get one too."

Christopher hesitated, his brow furrowing. "I don't even have an international passport, Sam. And honestly, I don't know if I have what it takes to apply for a visa."

Sam clapped him on the shoulder. "Come on, man. This is Nigeria. With a little help, you can get anything. Just imagine the potential! Plus, I can help you with the documents. Let's make it happen."

Sam's enthusiasm was infectious. Despite Christopher's doubts, Sam's words began to sink in.

Later, in a small café near the embassy, Sam leaned in and said, "Look, I know it sounds crazy, but with some money and the right connections, we can get you everything you need. You want to live a better life, right?"

Christopher nodded slowly. "I do. I really do. But I don't have a hefty bank account, or a job lined up. And I don't even know anyone in America."

Sam laughed. "That's why you have me! We'll get you an international passport, and I'll introduce you to someone who can help with the rest. You just need to take the first step."

As they chatted, Christopher began to warm up to the idea. Sam's optimism was a beacon in his uncertain world.

"How much do I need to get started?" Christopher asked, his voice tinged with cautious hope.

"Just put some money together," Sam advised. "Grease a few palms, and we'll get you sorted. It's a small price for the chance at a new life. Trust me, once you're abroad, this will all seem like chicken feed."

Christopher laughed. "Alright, Sam. Let's do this. I trust you."

With Sam's help, Christopher managed to get his international passport, investing a significant portion of his modest stipend in the process. Sam assured him that this was just the beginning, and with money and determination, anything was possible.

Christopher's journey was far from over. He needed to assemble a complex array of documents—proof of employment, a hefty bank balance, and evidence of ties to Nigeria. Despite the daunting tasks ahead, Sam's unwavering support and their shared hope for a brighter future fueled Christopher's resolve.

Ifeyinwa wasn't as easily convinced about the travel plans as Christopher had been. While Christopher's excitement and determination grew with each passing day, Ifeyinwa grappled with uncertainty. She had heard both the triumphs, and the harsh realities faced by foreigners striving to succeed abroad. The stories were filled with the promise of a better life, but also the arduous efforts required to achieve it.

"Chris are you sure about this?" she asked, her voice tinged with concern. "We don't have any close relatives in America. I've heard about how tough it can be for foreigners to make it there."

Christopher's eyes sparkled with unshaken resolve. "I know, but this is our chance. We've been struggling here, and I'm convinced that this is the only way forward for us. We must take this opportunity."

Despite her reservations, Ifeyinwa chose to support him. She began handing in over three-quarters of her salary each month to help with the visa process, entrusting the bulk of their finances to Christopher and his friend Sam.

Christopher was also buoyed by Sam's confident demeanor and his purported expertise in the "science" of visa procurement. Sam continuously regaled Christopher with detailed strategies, tips on answering interview questions, and even arranged for him to have mock interview sessions conducted by another expert, Mr. Odini in Agege.

When Sam returned from his second interview, he carried not the expected joy, but rejection slips and a stamp of refusal on his passport. His demeanor, however, remained oddly composed.

"Sam, what happened?" Christopher asked, struggling to mask his anxiety.

Sam shrugged, a half-smile on his face. "They didn't grant me the visa. But it's not the end. I've got a plan for reapplying and appealing. This is just a minor setback."

Christopher felt a pang of worry as he prepared for his own interview, scheduled a few weeks later. The day of the interview was tense. Dressed sharply in a crisp shirt, neatly tucked into his trousers, with a tie and polished shoes, he arrived at the embassy by 5 a.m., hoping for an early spot in the queue. His nerves were on edge as he watched other applicants with their impressive stacks of documents, some even buying spots in the line.

As the hours ticked by, Chris and the other hopefuls were eventually allowed into the embassy, where they were given numbers and directed to a waiting room. The anticipation was palpable. When Chris's number was finally called, he approached the counter with a mixture of trepidation and hope.

The official behind the counter looked at him with an unexpectedly friendly demeanor. "Hello," the official said without the grilling questions Chris had feared. "How long do you plan to stay in the U.S.? When do you intend to return?"

To this day, Chris is unable to recall his exact answers as he was that rattled. However, to his greatest surprise and utter disbelief, he was granted the visa. His joy was profound as he rushed out of the embassy, clutching the approval letter tightly. It felt like a dream come true.

He called Ifeyinwa, his voice barely containing his excitement.

"Ifeyinwa, you won't believe it! I got the visa! They approved it!"

Ifeyinwa's response was a mix of shock and elation. "Are you serious? This is incredible news, Chris!"

Christopher's excitement about the approved visa was tempered by his concern about traveling alone.

"Ifeyinwa," he said with earnest determination, "I can't do this alone. We've come this far together. You need to apply for a visa too."

Ifeyinwa was initially apprehensive but eventually agreed, knowing that their future together depended on it. The process of applying for the visa was fraught with its own set of anxieties and uncertainties. She immediately submitted her own application, and the waiting period was filled with nervous anticipation.

Then came the news she had hoped for but hardly dared to believe—her visa was approved. Her relief and joy were palpable. She called Christopher immediately, her voice filled with exhilaration. "Chris, it's official! I got the visa too!"

It was a double blessing for them. Their preparation for the journey to the U.S. got underway, and the excitement in their hearts grew with each passing day. They were about to step into a new life, a dream that had once seemed so far out of reach, now finally within their grasp.

As Ifeyinwa and Christopher packed their belongings in the small, well-worn room that had sheltered them for so many years, the weight of what was happening slowly began to sink in. The room, with its familiar peeling paint and creaky floorboards, felt suddenly foreign to them—like a memory they were preparing to leave behind.

"Ifeyinwa, can you believe it?" Christopher asked, holding up a battered old travel guide for the Tristate, flipping through the pages as though it contained the key to their future. "We're really going. It doesn't feel real yet."

Ifeyinwa paused, her fingers lingering on a stack of clothes she was folding. "I know," she said, a soft laugh escaping her. "I keep thinking someone's going to wake us up and tell us it was all a dream. Do you remember when we first started planning? I thought it was impossible— like we were chasing a dream too big for us."

"Impossible?" Christopher scoffed lightly, shaking his head as he set the guidebook down. "Sam had enough conviction for all of us. Do you remember how he used to talk about the States? He'd go on and on, like he could already see us there, living our best lives." His expression softened, and his voice lowered with a hint of sadness.

"Even though he didn't get the visa, he still introduced us to his relatives. They're ready to take us in when we arrive. He never stopped believing for us, even when it didn't work out for him."

Ifeyinwa's eyes filled with emotion. She set down the dress in her hands and turned toward Christopher, her voice tender. "Sam's been more than a friend. He's like a brother to us. I don't think we'd be this far without his help. His kindness, his unwavering faith... We owe him so much."

Christopher nodded, his face growing serious. "We'll never forget him or his kindness. I pray that he finally gets his visa in his next interview. If anyone deserves this chance, it's him—more than we do."

"He really does," Ifeyinwa said softly, her voice filled with gratitude. "When I think of how selfless he's been, always encouraging us when we were ready to give up... it hurts that he's still here, waiting."

Christopher's eyes glistened with a mix of hope and sorrow as he reached out to hold her hand. "His time will come, Ifeyinwa. I believe so with all my heart. And when it does, we'll be there waiting for him. We'll help him, just like he's helped us."

Ifeyinwa smiled through her emotions, squeezing Christopher's hand tightly. "We will. And when Sam finally gets off that plane, we'll be the first ones there to welcome him."

They stood in silence for a moment, holding each other in that small, dimly lit room, filled with memories of the past and the hope of their future. The sound of their packed suitcases and the shuffle of paper filled the room, but the weight of their shared gratitude and excitement for what lay ahead filled their hearts.

Soon after their arrival in the States, the initial euphoria of stepping onto American soil was quickly tempered by the cold, hard reality of their situation. The dream that had once seemed so full of promise now carried the weight of uncertainty.

They had entered the country on visiting visas, fully aware that their long-term plan had always been to stay indefinitely. But as the days turned into weeks, the stakes became painfully clear. Without securing permanent legal status, everything they had worked for—their sacrifices, their journey—would be for nothing.

The task ahead was daunting. Ifeyinwa and Christopher found themselves in a precarious position, navigating an unfamiliar system that was indifferent to their hopes and dreams. The fear of overstaying their visas, of slipping into the shadows of the undocumented, loomed over them like a dark cloud.

"We have to act fast," Christopher had said one evening, his voice low with concern as they sat in their cramped apartment, surrounded by boxes they had yet to unpack. "Without a clear path forward, all our efforts could be in vain."

Ifeyinwa, seated at the small kitchen table, stared at the visa documents spread before her. "I know," she whispered, the weight of their reality sinking in. "We can't afford to make any mistakes."

So began the arduous task of navigating their precarious situation. The first step was to sever ties with their past—a process that felt both emotionally and logistically complicated. They needed to initiate divorce proceedings, a legal formality to free themselves from their previous marital ties in Nigeria, making way for the next, more critical step: arranged marriages that would secure their immigration status.

"It feels... wrong," Ifeyinwa confessed one evening, her voice heavy with conflicted emotions. "To enter into a marriage just for papers. It feels like we're betraying everything we believe in."

Christopher looked at her, his expression serious but resigned. "I know it's not what we imagined, but what choice do we have? We must play the game if we want to stay here. We can't afford to let sentiment cloud our judgment."

They both knew the gravity of their decision. The process of finding suitable partners for these arranged marriages would be complex, involving legalities, paperwork, and a delicate dance of trust and negotiation. Every move they made had to be calculated, every step taken with care. The risk of failure hung over them constantly.

"It's just another part of the journey," Christopher had said, his tone determined despite the uncertainty. "We've made it this far. We'll get through this, too."

Ifeyinwa nodded, though her heart was heavy. "We have to. We didn't come all this way to give up now."

Their days became consumed by the legalities, consultations with immigration attorneys, and tense conversations with potential partners. Each new meeting, each new arrangement felt like walking a tightrope, knowing that one wrong step could send everything crashing down. It was a delicate balance between their hopes for the future and the cold, transactional nature of the path they were now forced to walk.

And so, they pressed on, knowing that this part of their journey was as complex as it was crucial—where love took a back seat to necessity, and every decision carried the weight of their future in a foreign land.

In the interim, Christopher found work as a cab operator, leveraging connections through Sam's relatives, who owned a small cab office. It wasn't the prestigious career he had once imagined for himself, but it offered something they desperately needed stability.

Every morning, he would wake up before dawn, tie his shoes with quiet determination, and head out into the city, navigating its sprawling streets and chaotic traffic, ferrying passengers from one point to another. It gave him a new sense of purpose and the comfort of a steady paycheck as they continued preparing for the next phase of their lives.

One evening, Christopher returned home after a long shift, his shoulders slumping with exhaustion but his eyes carrying a hint of pride.

"I picked up a businessman today," he said, dropping his keys onto the table. "He gave me a big tip. Said I reminded him of his younger days, hustling to make ends meet."

Ifeyinwa, who was preparing dinner in the small kitchen, smiled softly. "That's something, isn't it? You're working hard, and it's paying off."

"It's not much, but it's a start," Christopher replied, his voice filled with a quiet optimism. "We're moving forward, little by little."

Meanwhile, Ifeyinwa took her own steps toward building a foundation for their future. She had enrolled in a short course to become a Home Health Aide (HHA), a role that, while far from her dream career, would help them with their immediate financial needs. It was a steppingstone—one that would open doors, provide some income, and begin her journey in the U.S. healthcare system.

Each day, she balanced the demands of the course with the responsibilities of keeping their home in order, all while navigating the uncertainty of what lay ahead.

"This isn't where I thought I'd be," she confided to Christopher one night, her voice tinged with both hope and doubt. "But it's a start, right? One step closer to something bigger."

Christopher, sitting at the edge of the bed, gave her a reassuring look. "Exactly. It's not the destination; it's just the path we must take.

One day, you'll be in that hospital, wearing your white coat, and we'll look back on this as just another hurdle we overcame."

His words were a balm to her spirit, a reminder that their journey was far from over. They had already weathered many storms to get to this point—securing visas, finding jobs, navigating the labyrinth of immigration laws, and now, preparing for the most complicated and emotionally taxing part: their arranged marriages.

"Sometimes it feels like we're living in a movie," Ifeyinwa said with a half-smile. "A very complicated, dramatic movie."

Christopher chuckled softly. "Yeah, except we're the main characters, and we don't know how it's going to end."

They had managed to dissolve their marriage without drama, a legal formality that hadn't been easy but was necessary for their survival in the U.S.

Ifeyinwa had settled on a suitable partner, someone who understood the arrangement for what it was—strictly transactional. But Christopher's situation was more complicated.

His new partner, a sharp-eyed woman named Latoya, had made her conditions crystal clear. "We have to live together," she said flatly during their final meeting. Her tone was firm, leaving no room for negotiation. "No deal unless you move in."

Christopher had relayed the conversation to Ifeyinwa that night, his voice tense with frustration. "She's not budging. Either I move in with her, or the whole thing falls apart."

Ifeyinwa sat quietly for a moment, processing his words. "Do you think you can do it?" she asked softly, her heart heavy with the implications.

Christopher let out a deep sigh, running a hand through his hair. "It's not ideal, but we don't have a choice, do we? If I don't go through with it, everything we've built here could come crashing down."

"I know," she replied, her voice steady but filled with unspoken emotion. "It's just... hard. We've come so far together, and now..."

"Ife, this is temporary," Christopher interrupted gently, his hand finding hers. "We're doing this to survive. To stay here, to build a future. It doesn't change anything between us."

She nodded, though the reality of the situation weighed heavily on her. They had sacrificed so much, endured so many trials to get to this point, and now they were forced to take this next step—one that tested not only their resolve but the depth of their bond.

As they navigated these new challenges, their focus remained firmly on their goals of establishing themselves in America and turning their dreams into reality. Their journey had been a mosaic of hope, struggle, and relentless pursuit of a better life. Each day brought its own set of hurdles, but they faced them with the same determination that had carried them across oceans and through the uncertainty of immigration.

Together, they resolved to press forward, knowing that no matter what obstacles lay ahead, they would face them head-on. For in the end, this was not just about survival—it was about building a future where they could truly thrive.

Yet, amidst the whirlwind of their new reality, Ifeyinwa found herself grappling with a profound uncertainty. The glittering promise of the American dream had come at a cost—one that weighed heavily on her, especially in the quiet moments when she was alone.

The sacrifices they had made were significant, but some days, the weight of those sacrifices felt heavier than she had anticipated.

She had always imagined that the transition to life in the U.S. would be hard, but nothing could have prepared her for the loneliness she felt during her first pregnancy.

Christopher had been around in the beginning, visiting whenever he could, but as time passed, those visits became less frequent. He was wrapped up in his own struggles, navigating the convoluted web of immigration while trying to keep up appearances with Latoya.

"I thought by now, things would be different," Ifeyinwa whispered one night, sitting on the edge of the bed, her hand resting protectively on her swollen belly. She had just put their first child, Ofor to sleep, and the silence of the house only amplified her thoughts.

As she rubbed her belly, feeling the soft movements of their second child, growing inside her, she couldn't help but wonder when—if ever—Christopher would come back home for good. "By the time She is born, he'll be home," she had told herself repeatedly during those long months. But the reality was far different. His papers were still tied up in endless bureaucracy, and though hers had come through, Christopher's future remained uncertain.

One day, as she stood in the kitchen, preparing a simple meal, the phone rang. It was Christopher. His voice, though familiar, felt distant—like a fading echo of the man who had once been her constant support.

"How are things?" he asked, his tone light but strained.

"Fine," she replied, stirring the pot absentmindedly. "The baby is growing fast. I think she'll be here sooner than we expected."

"That's good," Christopher said, but there was hesitation in his voice that Ifeyinwa couldn't ignore.

"When will you come home?" she asked quietly, the question hanging in the air between them like a fragile thread.

There was a pause at the other end. "Soon," he finally answered. "I'm still waiting for my papers. It's taking longer than I thought. But I'll be there, Ife. I promise."

Ifeyinwa's grip tightened on the spoon, the weight of his words pressing down on her. She had heard this promise before—over and over again. Each time, she wanted to believe him, to hold on to the hope that he would walk through the door and be with her, to raise their children together. But as the months turned into years, that hope was beginning to fray.

"You always say that." She murmured, her voice barely above a whisper.

Christopher sighed, his frustration evident. "I'm trying, Ife. You know I am. This process—it's not in my hands. I'm doing everything I can."

"I know," she replied, though the ache in her heart told a different story. "But it's hard, Christopher. Being here, alone... raising one child and about to have another... it's not what I imagined."

"I didn't imagine this either," he said quietly. "I didn't think it would be this hard. But we're close, Ife. Just hold on a little longer."

"I'm holding on," she whispered, tears stinging her eyes. "But it feels like I'm holding on to nothing sometimes."

The line went quiet for a moment, and Ifeyinwa felt the weight of their situation settle in once again. This wasn't the life they had envisioned when they set out on their journey to America. They had dreamed of a fresh start, a life of opportunity and prosperity. But the reality had been so much harder—lonelier.

After the call ended, Ifeyinwa sat in silence for a long time, staring at the pot on the stove. She had never imagined that she would have to go through this alone, that she would give birth to their second child without Christopher by her side. She thought about all the milestones he had missed, the first steps of their eldest, the sound of their first words. Now, with their daughter on the way, she feared he would miss even more.

"How much longer?" she whispered to herself, feeling the exhaustion settle deep in her bones. How much longer could she wait for him, for their family to finally come together?

She rubbed her belly again, feeling the baby's soft kicks, and forced herself to hold on to the hope she still had. Because what other choice did, she have? This was the life they had chosen, the path they had committed to. And though the road had been far from easy,

Ifeyinwa knew she couldn't give up—not on herself, not on her children, and not on Christopher. Even when the distance between them felt insurmountable, she had to believe that one day, it would all be worth it.

She often allowed herself at her weakest moments to lament about the contrast between her idyllic childhood in Aba and the whirlwind of her current life. The simplicity of her past seemed a world away from the intricate dance of legalities and the relentless pursuit of stability in a foreign land. The dream of a better future had come at a significant cost, and she sometimes wondered if the price had been too high.

Their once-clear vision of success in America now appeared muddled with the challenges of living apart, the intricacies of their legal maneuvers, and the strain of their new jobs. Despite the initial excitement and the early successes, Ifeyinwa couldn't shake the nagging doubt that perhaps the journey had altered the very essence of what they had hoped to achieve.

CLARA

As Clara walked back to her home after seeing Ifeyinwa off to her car, her thoughts were filled with the warmth of the evening yet tinged with bittersweet longing. The last time she and her friends had all gathered in one place felt like a distant memory, and she missed them deeply.

"They're like my sisters," she whispered to herself, her voice carrying softly in the quiet neighborhood. "Even though we're scattered across the globe, our bond keeps us close."

She paused at the front of the two-bedroom townhouse she shared with her husband, Emeka, and bent over to tug at a persistent weed poking out between the slabs on their side of the common porch. As she straightened, her eyes instinctively drifted two doors down. There she was—Mrs. Hawk, just as Clara expected.

"Of course, she's there," Clara muttered, standing up fully and squinting slightly. Mrs. Hawk, the petite elderly woman with heavily rimmed glasses and sparse hair tied in a neat bun, was perched at her usual spot by the window.

Clara stared directly at her, but Mrs. Hawk didn't so much as twitch. It was like trying to make eye contact with a statue—eerie and unyielding.

"Does she ever get tired?" Clara mused, half-amused, half-uneasy.

"Does she ever leave that spot?"

She imagined the old woman with a notebook on her lap, diligently recording the comings and goings of everyone in the neighborhood. Maybe she even had a log of Clara's routine, neatly jotted down in small, precise handwriting.

"Page 42: Clara and Emeka went grocery shopping at 5 PM," Clara said to herself, her tone half-joking. "Page 43: New neighbor took a strange midnight walk."

The thought of Mrs. Hawk keeping tabs on everyone made Clara chuckle nervously, but there was a hint of discomfort behind the laughter. She had considered waving or saying hello several times but always hesitated.

"Remember that first time," Clara whispered to herself, the memory as clear as day. It was shortly after she had arrived in the U.S. to join Emeka. She had been so eager to fit in, to make friends, to be a good neighbor. One afternoon, she walked past Mrs. Hawk's window and decided to greet her.

"Good afternoon, Ma'am!" she had called out, the words rolling off her tongue with the crispness Emeka had taught her. But she still remembered how strange it had felt to say "Ma'am" instead of the "Madam" she was used to back home in Nigeria.

"Why do they drop the 'd'?" Clara had asked Emeka once, confused by the pronunciation. "It's like they're stuttering."

"This is America," Emeka had replied with a laugh. "Things are different here, and you'll get used to it."

So, she had practiced until it felt natural. But when she called out to Mrs. Hawk that day, the response—or lack of it—had caught her off guard.

There had been no reaction, not even a flicker of acknowledgment from Mrs. Hawk. The silence that followed was colder than the winter air that day. Clara had felt an unexpected sting, as if she had been deliberately ignored.

"Not even a nod," Clara said now, recalling the moment with a small frown. "Just sitting there, like a hawk, watching, waiting."

From that day on, she had mentally dubbed the woman Mrs. Hawk. The name fit her too well, a sharp-eyed, ever-watchful presence that seemed to miss nothing. But the lack of any acknowledgment had left Clara feeling both puzzled and a little hurt.

"Maybe she's just shy," Clara thought, her heart softening momentarily. "Or maybe… she just doesn't know how to reach out."

But just as quickly, she dismissed the thought. "Or maybe she's just content watching, like a hawk biding its time."

She stared back at the window one last time before turning away with a small sigh. The connection she had once hoped for with Mrs. Hawk seemed more elusive than ever, but the curiosity lingered.

"Who knows," Clara muttered as she reached for her keys. "Maybe one day she'll say something. Or maybe I'll try again… if I can find the nerve."

But for now, Clara knew she would continue to greet Mrs. Hawk with just a glance, just like always.

If there was one thing that unsettled Clara about living in America, it was the fate of the elderly as she foresaw it. Take Mrs. Hawk, for example. The petite, elderly white lady spent most of her days sitting at her window, silently watching the world go by. To Clara, it seemed like Mrs. Hawk was watching life itself slowly slip away.

"One day, they'll probably cart her off to a nursing home," Clara thought, a wave of sadness washing over her. "She'll die alone, surrounded by strangers."

Clara couldn't help but imagine how different Mrs. Hawk's life could have been if she lived back home, in Clara's village. She pictured Mrs. Hawk in a kindred home, surrounded by family, children running around, and the chatter of relatives filling the air. It would be a life full of warmth and companionship, not the lonely existence of a silent observer.

"She'd be attending age-grade meetings, church services, and ceremonies," Clara murmured to herself, her heart heavy with the contrast. "There wouldn't be a dull moment with plenty of kin around her."

The thought of Mrs. Hawk being consigned to a nursing home, isolated from everything familiar, made Clara shudder. It was an existence she couldn't bear to imagine for herself or anyone she loved.

"No," Clara thought firmly, her resolve hardening. "Emeka and I will build our retirement home back home. We'll buy the land, construct the house, and make sure it's furnished and equipped for our old age."

The idea of being placed in a nursing home among strangers was something Clara couldn't fathom. The thought alone made her visibly shudder as she reentered her apartment, shutting the door behind her with a finality that echoed her trepidation.

As the door clicked shut, the apartment felt eerily quiet, the remnants of laughter and chatter from her friends now a distant memory. The silence was almost oppressive after the lively gathering earlier.

Clara sighed and began tidying up, clearing the glasses and plates that had been used to entertain her guests. She carried them to the kitchen sink, where she placed them to be washed later. With methodical precision, she wiped down the tables, dusted the surfaces, and vacuumed the lounge.

Glancing at the clock on the kitchen wall, she realized it was almost 4 PM. "Emeka will be home soon," she thought, a soft smile playing on her lips. It was time to start preparing his dinner. He liked the house to be neat and a freshly prepared meal waiting for him when he returned from work. Clara had never failed him and had no intention of starting now.

As she began gathering ingredients for dinner, she felt a deep sense of contentment. "I don't mind catering to his needs," she mused. "People may think I'm submissive, but they don't know us. They don't know what we've been through."

Her devotion to Emeka was unwavering. "His word is my command," she would readily tell anyone who dared to question her obvious devotion. She didn't care what others thought; they couldn't understand the bond she shared with her husband. Emeka had saved her family from a dark time, and for that, she would forever be grateful.

As Clara continued preparing dinner, her mind drifted to thoughts of her mother—a woman of remarkable strength who had single-handedly raised Clara and her older brother, Adindu. Her father's memory was nothing more than a blurred photograph and stories told by others, for he had died in a tragic motor accident just a year after she was born.

"I never knew him," Clara whispered, her voice tinged with a sorrow she rarely allowed herself to feel. But her mother, oh, how she had known hardship and yet never let it break her.

Clara's hands paused momentarily as she recalled the stories her mother had shared, often late at night when the world was quiet, and it was just the two of them sitting by the dim light of a kerosene lamp. Her mother had spoken of the battles she had faced after her father's death—battles that Clara, even as a child, could scarcely comprehend.

"When your father died," her mother had said, "your uncle tried to claim me as his wife."

Clara remembered the way her mother's voice had hardened at the mention of her father's younger brother. It was tradition in their culture for a son to inherit his father's wives, excluding his birth mother, of course. But it had never been the norm for a brother to claim his sibling's widow.

"He wanted me not out of love or duty," her mother had continued, her tone laced with bitterness, "but because I was doing well with the yam trade. He saw my success and wanted to take advantage of it."

Clara could still see her mother's stern face in those moments, the way her jaw set in defiance as she recounted how she had resisted her brother-in-law's advances. No one in the family had intervened, and her uncle's intentions became clear when his coercion turned to slander.

"He started spreading rumors," her mother had said, her eyes blazing with a mix of anger and pain. "He called me a witch, blamed me for your father's death."

The cruelty of it all had struck young Clara deeply. The man who should have protected them had instead become their greatest adversary. The situation grew so unbearable that her mother had no choice but to flee the town, taking Clara and Adindu with her to a neighboring village.

"She was a survivor," Clara murmured now, feeling a swell of pride mixed with sadness. Her mother had resumed her yam trade, but it was never the same. The distance had cost her the loyal customers and farmers she once had, and their lives became a daily struggle.

Clara could still remember the day her mother broke the news to her. She had been sitting outside their modest home, trying to concentrate on her schoolwork, when her mother approached with a heavy heart.

"Clara, my dear," her mother began, her voice tinged with sadness. "I won't be able to send you to the university."

The words hit Clara like a physical blow. She had always known money was tight, but she had clung to the hope that somehow, they would find a way. But now, hearing her mother say it out loud made it real.

"But Mama," Clara had protested, her voice quivering with emotion, "I've worked so hard. I thought … …."

"I know, my child," her mother interrupted gently, her eyes filling with tears. "But with Adindu already in university, there's just no money left. Unless we start stealing, which we will not do, I don't see how we can manage it."

Clara had nodded, swallowing the lump in her throat. She was heartbroken, but she knew her mother was right. They were good people; they wouldn't resort to dishonesty to achieve their dreams.

Days passed, and Clara tried to come to terms with her fate. Then, unexpectedly, a lifeline appeared from the most unlikely source.

Their landlady had always admired how well-behaved Clara and Adindu were. She had often spoken to her son, who lived in America, about Clara, encouraging him to come home and meet her.

"He should marry a good girl like Clara," the landlady would say proudly. "She's well-mannered, beautiful, and comes from a respectable family."

When the son finally returned home, he was eager to meet this Clara his mother had spoken so highly of. But when he did, he found himself conflicted. Clara was indeed everything his mother had described, but she was also young—too young, he thought, for marriage.

Still, he couldn't shake the impression she had made on him. There was something about her—a quiet dignity, a strength of character—that drew him in. So, he devised a plan.

He asked his mother to invite Clara over one day, making sure to be in the next room where he could hear their conversation without being seen. As they spoke, Clara's voice drifted through the walls—soft, yet steady and full of resolve. He listened closely, each word affirming what he had already sensed about her.

"This is a girl with strength," he thought to himself. "She deserves more than what life has handed her."

Clara spoke about her struggles, how hard it had been to balance work and home, and the dreams she had quietly kept alive in the back of her mind. As she spoke, her voice held a quiet grit that captivated him.

"I can help her," he thought. "She just needs a chance."

After their meeting ended, he made up his mind. He would offer to pay for her college education, with no strings attached. If, after she graduated, she wanted to marry him, they would. But if not, there would be no pressure—no expectations. It was a risk, but one he was more than willing to take.

The next day, Clara's landlady approached her with the news. The offer left Clara completely stunned.

"But why would he do this for me?" Clara asked, her voice laced with disbelief. "I don't even know him like that. Why would anyone invest in my future with no expectation of anything in return?"

The landlady smiled gently, placing a hand on Clara's shoulder. "Because he sees your potential, Clara. He believes in you."

Clara shook her head, still unable to fully grasp it. "But... what if I can't pay him back? What if I never … …."

The landlady cut her off. "There are no strings, my dear. He's not asking for repayment. He just wants to give you an opportunity. The rest is up to you."

Clara stood there, the weight of the decision pressing heavily on her chest. It felt surreal, too good to be true.

"But people don't just do things like this," Clara murmured, more to herself than anyone else.

"Some people do," the landlady replied softly. "And you deserve it."

Clara sat down, overwhelmed. The offer was so generous—so life-changing—that it almost frightened her. Would she be able to live up to the faith he had in her? Could she accept something so significant without feeling obligated?

As she pondered, one thought stood out clearly in her mind: For the first time in her life, someone saw beyond her circumstances and believed in her potential. Perhaps, she thought, this was the chance she had been waiting for all along.

And so, Clara's life took a new turn. For four years, she attended university, supported not only financially but emotionally as well. Her benefactor was true to his words; he never demanded anything of her, never pressured her in any way. Instead, he extended his generosity to her family, helping her brother and mother as well.

Clara worked hard in those years, driven not just by her own dreams, but by the deep gratitude she felt toward the man who had given her a second chance. And though she knew that the possibility of marriage loomed in the distance, she also knew that whatever her decision, it would be hers alone.

After her graduation, Emeka returned as promised, this time not just as the kind benefactor who had supported her education, but as a man deeply in love and ready to spend the rest of his life with her. He had seen her grow from a bright, hopeful young woman into a confident and educated lady, and his feelings for her had only deepened over the years.

A week later, on a warm afternoon, Emeka invited Clara to a quiet spot near the river. The sun was setting, casting a golden glow over the water.

"Clara," Emeka began, his voice gentle but firm, "I've watched you grow into an incredible woman. You've worked so hard, and I couldn't be prouder of you."

Clara smiled, feeling a warmth spread through her chest. "I couldn't have done it without you, Emeka. You've been my rock, my biggest supporter."

Emeka took a deep breath, his heart pounding. "Clara, I've loved you from the moment I met you. I didn't say anything then because I wanted you to have your own future, to make your own choices. But now… now I want to build that future with you."

He reached into his pocket and pulled out a small velvet box, opening it to reveal a simple, elegant ring. "Clara, will you marry me?"

Tears welled up in Clara's eyes. She had dreamed of this moment, but hearing the words, seeing the ring, it all felt so surreal. "Emeka… yes, yes, I'll marry you," she said, her voice trembling with emotion.

Emeka slipped the ring onto her finger, then pulled her into a tight embrace. "You've made me the happiest man in the world," he whispered into her ear.

Their wedding was a few months later, a joyous occasion that brought together friends and family. On the morning of the ceremony, Clara stood in front of the mirror, adjusting her veil. She turned to Emeka's mother, who had become like a second mother to her.

"Do you think he'll like the dress?" Clara asked, her nerves getting the best of her.

Emeka's mother smiled warmly. "My dear, Emeka will love anything you wear, but more than that, he loves you. That's all that matters."

When Clara walked down the aisle, her eyes met Emeka's, and everything else faded away. As she reached him, he took her hands in his, his voice filled with emotion as he said, "You look beautiful, Clara. I'm so lucky to have you by my side."

He looked at her with such adoration that everyone present could see just how much he cherished her.

Clara blushed, her heart swelling with love. "I'm the lucky one, Emeka. You've given me everything I could have ever asked for."

After the ceremony, as they danced together under the twinkling lights, Emeka leaned in and whispered, "This is just the beginning, my love. We have a lifetime of happiness ahead of us."

Clara nodded, resting her head on his chest, feeling the steady beat of his heart. "I can't wait to start our life together, Emeka. I promise to make you as happy as you've made me."

The transition to married life was seamless for Clara. Emeka, who had lived in the USA for over 20 years, had already prepared everything for her arrival. The day she stepped off the plane, he was there, waiting with open arms and a beaming smile.

"Welcome home, my love," Emeka said warmly as he pulled her into a tight embrace.

Clara smiled at him, feeling a sense of peace wash over her. "It feels good to be here," she whispered, already feeling the love and safety his presence always brought.

Their new home was in a peaceful neighborhood, with tree-lined streets and a quiet, welcoming atmosphere in Brooklyn. Emeka had thought of everything, from the cozy furnishings to the fully stocked kitchen. As they walked through the front door, Clara was overwhelmed with emotion.

"You've done so much for me already," Clara said, her eyes welling up. "I don't even know where to start thanking you."

Emeka cupped her face gently, brushing a tear from her cheek. "You don't need to thank me. This is our life now, Clara. I just want you to be happy here."

Clara smiled and nodded. "I already am."

Emeka guided her through the process of acclimating to her new country with patience and encouragement. He taught her how to navigate the city, helped her get her driver's license, and supported her as she began pursuing her own dreams. But despite the adjustments, their marriage was blissful from the very start.

In the mornings, Clara would rise early to prepare breakfast, making sure Emeka's favorite meals were always on the table. One day, after setting down his plate of akara and pap, she sat beside him, watching with eager anticipation as he took the first bite.

"Mmm," Emeka hummed in satisfaction. "You spoil me, Clara."

She laughed, her heart swollen with joy. "I just want to make sure my husband is happy."

"You do more than that," he replied, reaching out to squeeze her hand. "You make me the happiest man alive."

Emeka never took Clara's efforts for granted. He showed his appreciation in countless ways—whether it was surprising her with a bouquet of flowers or whisking her away for a weekend getaway.

One evening, after they had returned from a short trip to the coast, Clara snuggled into Emeka's side on the couch, their fingers intertwined.

"Can you believe we've been married for almost three years?" Clara asked, her voice soft with contentment.

"I can," Emeka replied, kissing the top of her head. "But it feels like we've just begun. I feel like I fall in love with you more every day."

Clara smiled, looking up at him. "I feel the same way. I never thought life could be this perfect."

They spent their evenings like this—talking about the future, making plans for the family they hoped to have one day, and dreaming about the places they'd visit together. They were partners in every sense of the word, supporting each other through every high and low.

One night, as they lay in bed after a long day, Clara turned to Emeka with a thoughtful expression.

"Thank you," she said softly.

"For what?" Emeka asked, turning to face her.

"For everything. For this life. For being such a wonderful husband. I don't think I could ever love anyone the way I love you."

Emeka smiled and gently pulled her closer. "I should be the one thanking you, Clara. You've made this house a home. I'm the luckiest man alive."

As time passed, a subtle emptiness began to creep into Clara and Emeka's otherwise perfect life. It started as a quiet, unspoken longing, but soon it became impossible to ignore.

At first, neither of them mentioned it directly. They continued their lives, filling their home with laughter, shared meals, and loving gestures. But every time Clara saw a mother pushing a stroller down their peaceful street or heard a baby's soft coos in a grocery store, a pang of yearning welled up inside her. She knew Emeka felt it too, though he rarely spoke about it.

One evening, after they had finished dinner, Clara sat at the kitchen table, absentmindedly tracing patterns on the wood surface with her finger. Emeka noticed her silence and came to sit beside her, gently placing his hand over hers.

"Clara, what's on your mind?" he asked softly.

She hesitated, her eyes welling up with unshed tears. "I'm happy, Emeka. I really am. But..." She took a deep breath. "I feel like something's missing. I know we've been trying, but it's been so long, and … …." her voice cracked slightly. "What if it never happens for us?"

Emeka looked at her with a mix of tenderness and concern. He had always been her rock, but even he couldn't hide the pain in his eyes.

"We'll keep trying," he said, his voice steady but laced with the same fear. "But Clara, you have to know—you are enough for me. No matter what happens, I love you, and I always will."

Clara nodded, wiping a tear from her cheek. "I know," she whispered. "And I love you too. I just… I want to be able to give you a family."

"You've already given me a family, Clara," Emeka said softly. "You and me—that's a family."

Despite his comforting words, the ache inside Clara continued to grow. Everything still appeared perfect on the outside, but inside, Clara battled a storm of emotions. She couldn't shake the feeling that she was failing him, failing them.

Emeka noticed the strain Clara was under and did his best to lighten her burden. "Clara," he would say, taking her hand gently, "we have each other. That's what matters most. We can still live a fulfilling life together, with or without a child."

Clara would nod, forcing a smile, but deep down, she couldn't let go of the feeling that she was letting him down. She began to withdraw from friends and family, not wanting to face their pity or, worse, their unsolicited advice. The stress of it all started to take a toll on her, both physically and emotionally

One night, as they lay in bed, Clara turned to Emeka, her voice barely above a whisper. "Do you think we'll ever get our miracle?"

Emeka wrapped his arms around her, holding her tightly. "I don't know," he admitted. "But I do know that we're strong enough to face whatever comes. Together."

Clara rested her head against his chest, listening to the steady beat of his heart. She wanted to believe that, despite the challenges they were facing, they would find peace—whether it came in the form of a child or in the quiet acceptance of their love.

As she closed her eyes, she whispered, "I love you, Emeka. More than anything."

Emeka kissed her forehead softly. "I love you too, Clara. More than you'll ever know."

They spent the following years navigating the maze of alternative treatments and measures, consultations and endless prayers, but to no avail. With time, Clara's hope began to wane, and every monthly disappointment felt like a blow to her heart. The pressure mounted, and the once joyful Clara became a shadow of her former self.

With five years gone and no pregnancy, Clara knew she had to make a drastic decision. They decided to consult with fertility specialists in the hopes of finding some clarity.

One afternoon, as they sat in the specialist's office, Clara felt the tension in the air. She glanced at Emeka, who offered her a reassuring smile, but she could see her similar worry behind his eyes.

The doctor entered, holding their latest test results. "Alright, let's go over your reports," he began, settling into his chair. "Clara, everything looks mostly normal. There is a small fibroid, but it's not in a location that should interfere with your ability to conceive."

Clara sighed, her shoulders relaxing slightly. "So, it's not the fibroid then?"

The doctor shook his head. "No, I don't believe the fibroid is the cause. Many women live with fibroids and still conceive without any issues. Your other tests came back normal—no signs of blocked tubes or hormonal imbalances."

The doctor then turned to Emeka. "Emeka, your sperm count is lower than average. It's not severely low, but it could be a contributing factor. However, with assisted reproductive techniques like intrauterine insemination (IUI) or in vitro fertilization (IVF), there's a good chance you can still conceive."

Emeka nodded slowly. "So, it's not impossible?"

"Not impossible at all," the doctor said, leaning forward. "It's just a little more complicated. We could start you on medication to help boost your count, and from there, we can explore IVF if you're open to it."

Clara and Emeka exchanged a glance, silently weighing their options.

"I think we should try everything," Clara said after a moment, her voice determined. "I want to give us the best chance."

Emeka nodded, squeezing her hand. "We'll do whatever it takes."

Months passed, filled with medications, monitoring cycles, and endless tests. Clara underwent hormone injections, and Emeka changed his lifestyle to improve his sperm count, but each IVF cycle ended the same way—with no pregnancy.

One evening, after another failed round, Clara sat on the couch with her head in her hands. "What are we doing wrong, Emeka?" she whispered, her voice breaking.

Emeka sat beside her, his arm around her shoulders. "We're not doing anything wrong, love. Some things… they just take time."

"But it's been years," Clara said, tears streaming down her face. "What if we never have a baby?"

Emeka pulled her closer, his voice soft but steady. "Then we'll still have each other, Clara. We've been through so much already. We'll get through this too."

Despite Emeka's reassurances, the weight of the situation bore heavily on Clara. She felt like time was slipping through her fingers, and with each passing month, the void in their lives grew larger.

After yet another consultation, the doctor's words rang in her ears: "Everything points to the sperm count, but sometimes the body surprises us. It's possible there's another factor we haven't pinpointed."

That night, Clara lay awake, staring at the ceiling, her mind racing with possibilities. Then, a thought came to her—one she had been avoiding.

The next morning, Clara broached the topic over breakfast.

"Emeka," she began, pushing her plate aside, "I've been thinking… about the fibroid."

Emeka looked up from his coffee, his brow furrowed. "The fibroid? But the doctors said it's not a problem."

"I know," Clara said, her voice steady but filled with uncertainty.

"But it's the only thing left we haven't addressed. What if they're wrong? What if removing it could make a difference?"

Emeka leaned back in his chair, thinking. "Clara, I don't want you to go through surgery if it's unnecessary. The doctors were clear—it's not causing the issue."

"I understand that," Clara said, her hands trembling slightly. "But I feel like I need to try this. I can't help but wonder if it's the reason we're not conceiving. And I can't live with that 'what if.'"

Emeka reached across the table, taking her hand. "If you truly believe this will help, then we'll do it. But please know, Clara, you don't have to go through this for me. I love you, no matter what happens."

Clara smiled weakly, her eyes misting over. "I know, Emeka. But I need to do this—for us, for myself. I want to give us every possible chance."

Emeka sighed deeply, his thumb stroking the back of her hand.

"Then we'll do it," he said quietly. "But only if, you're sure."

"I am," Clara nodded, her resolve strengthening. "I'm sure."

They sat in silence for a moment, the weight of the decision settling over them both. The room was dimly lit, and the hum of the city outside seemed far away, like a world they no longer belonged to. Their life had become consumed by this single, agonizing quest for a child, and now, Clara was ready to take the next step, even if it meant going under the knife.

A few days later, Clara met with the doctor to discuss the procedure. The surgeon explained the risks, but Clara's mind was already made up. She scheduled the surgery for the following month.

On the morning of the surgery, as Clara lay in the hospital bed, waiting to be taken into the operating room, Emeka sat beside her, holding her hand tightly. His face was calm, but his eyes betrayed the worry he felt.

"You're going to be fine," he whispered, brushing a strand of hair from her face.

Clara smiled weakly. "I know. I'm ready."

As the nurses came to wheel her away, Emeka kissed her forehead. "I love you, Clara. No matter what happens, we'll get through this."

Clara nodded, her heart swelling with love and fear all at once. "I love you too, Emeka. More than anything."

ADAOBI

Adaobi's life was the perfect fusion of American pop culture and the Nigerian values her parents held onto so tightly. Born and bred in the Bronx, she was as American as apple pie—though, in her case, it was more like pizza slices and hip-hop beats. Her father held down a steady job at CVS, while her mother's long shifts as a nurse made sure there was always food on the table. The streets of New York were her playground, and the city's heartbeat was in sync with hers.

From a young age, Adaobi soaked in everything around her—the late-night bodegas, the endless stream of yellow cabs, the graffiti-streaked subway cars, and the unmistakable pulse of New York City. She was a true Bronx girl, repping her borough with pride. She could rap along to every Queen Latifah verse, knew the best spots to get chopped cheese, and had mastered the art of side-eyeing anyone who dared to look at her funny on the train.

But as she hit high school, her parents started to worry. Adaobi was diving headfirst into the American teenage experience, and they feared she was losing touch with the Nigerian culture they had fought so hard to maintain. She was spending more time hanging out with her friends after school, jamming to the latest Jay-Z album, and less time at the family dinners where her mother served jollof rice and told stories about life back in the village.

Adaobi's descent into the depths of American teenage culture was swift and, in her parents' eyes, alarming. She had always been a good girl—polite, studious, and respectful—but high school in the Bronx was a different beast. The allure of fitting in, of being part of the crowd, started to pull her away from the values her parents had worked so hard to instill.

It all came to a head one Friday night. Adaobi had asked her parents if she could spend the night at her friend Rachel's house. Rachel lived just a few blocks away, and her parents were strict, so Adaobi's parents didn't think twice before giving their consent. Little did they know that Rachel's older brother was throwing a party—a rave, as they called it and was far from the innocent sleepover they'd imagined.

The night was a blur of pounding music, flashing lights, and the heady mix of alcohol and smoke. Adaobi found herself swept up in the thrill of it all, dancing to the bass-heavy beats and laughing with friends. Someone passed her a joint, and though she hesitated for a moment, the pressure to fit in pushed her to take a puff. The rest of the night passed in a hazy mix of excitement and rebellion, with Adaobi feeling like she was finally a part of something bigger, something undeniably American.

When she finally made it home the next morning, still groggy and with a slight headache, she hoped to sneak past her parents unnoticed. But as soon as she walked through the door, her mother's sharp eyes caught something amiss.

"Adaobi," her mother called out from the kitchen, "come here, please."

Adaobi's heart raced. She knew that tone. It was the one her mother used when she was about to ask a question, she already knew the answer to. Trying to stay calm, Adaobi walked into the kitchen, her hands shoved deep into her pockets.

"Yes, Mom?" she asked, her voice as casual as she could manage.

Her mother looked up from where she was stirring a pot of stew, her nose wrinkling slightly as Adaobi got closer.

"What's that smell?"

Adaobi's heart sank. "What smell?" she asked, feigning ignorance, though she knew exactly what her mother was referring to.

"That smell," her mother insisted, narrowing her eyes. "It smells like… like marijuana. Adaobi, where were you last night?"

Adaobi fumbled for an answer, her mind racing. "I was at Rachel's… we just hung out, watched movies…"

Her mother's face hardened. "Don't lie to me, Adaobi. I wasn't born yesterday."

At that moment, her father walked into the kitchen, sensing the tension. He took one look at Adaobi and his face fell. "What's going on here?" he asked, his voice low and filled with concern.

"Adaobi's clothes smell like marijuana," her mother said flatly, her gaze never leaving her daughter's face.

Her father's expression darkened, and Adaobi could see the disappointment in his eyes. "Adaobi, is this true? Were you at a party?"

Adaobi bit her lips, feeling trapped. She had always hated lying to her parents, but the truth seemed just as unbearable. "It wasn't like that," she finally said, her voice small. "It was just a party, nothing bad happened…"

"Nothing bad?" her father echoed, his voice rising in anger. "Do you think smelling like marijuana is nothing bad? Do you realize what could have happened to you?"

Adaobi hung her head, tears welling up in her eyes. She knew she had messed up, but she hadn't expected this level of disappointment. "I'm sorry," she whispered, but the words felt hollow.

Her parents exchanged a look, one that spoke volumes. They had been worried for a while now, but this was the final straw. That evening, they sat Adaobi down, along with her younger brother, Onisa, and delivered the news that would change her life.

"You're going to Nigeria," her father announced, his tone brooking no argument. "Both of you. You need to reconnect with your roots, learn what it means to be Nigerian."

Adaobi stared at them, her mouth agape. "Nigeria? But… why? I'm fine here! I made a mistake, but I can fix it!"

Her mother shook her head, her expression a mix of sadness and determination. "This isn't just about fixing a mistake, Adaobi. It's about understanding who you are and where you come from. We've made our decision."

Adaobi continued to protest. "Nigeria? You want to send me away? But everything I know is here! My friends, school… New York is my home!"

Her mother's eyes softened, but her resolve didn't waver. "This isn't about taking you away from what you know. It's about giving you the chance to connect with your heritage. You'll learn things in Nigeria that you can't learn here."

"But what about prom? What about college applications? I'm supposed to be thinking about SATs, not learning how to speak Igbo fluently!" Adaobi's voice was rising, a mix of fear and frustration.

Her father stepped closer, his gaze steady. "Adaobi, you're more than just what's here. This is your chance to find out who you really are, where you really come from."

The weight of their words finally settled over Adaobi like a heavy blanket. She wanted to argue some more, to beg them to let her stay, but deep down, she knew it was useless. The party, the marijuana—it had all been too much for them. And now, she was being sent away, far from the life she had always known.

Adaobi could still remember the day they first stepped off the plane at Muritala Mohammed Airport. The air was thick with heat, unlike the cool breeze of New York. As soon as they exited the airport, the cacophony of unfamiliar accents hit them, a far cry from the familiar hum of the Bronx. The streets were alive with movement—people hustling about, vendors calling out their wares, and taxis honking incessantly. It was like stepping into a different world, one that felt completely alien to her.

"Is it always this hot?" Onisa muttered, tugging at his collar. He was barely twelve, but the look on his face was that of someone far older, someone who had just realized the world was much bigger and more overwhelming than he had ever imagined.

Adaobi nodded, too stunned to speak. She glanced around, noting with a start that, for the first time in her life, she was surrounded by a sea of black faces. In New York, diversity was the norm, but here, it was as if she had finally come face to face with the essence of who she was supposed to be. Yet, it felt strange, unfamiliar, and a bit intimidating.

The week before they were due to head to boarding school was spent in Oguta, their parents' hometown.

It was a small town, nothing like the bustling cityscapes Adaobi was used to. The roads were narrower, the buildings older, and the air was thick with the scent of earth and vegetation.

"Look, Adaobi, look at that!" Onisa's voice broke into her thoughts as he pointed excitedly to a large, brightly colored cockerel strutting around the compound.

Adaobi's eyes widened. She had seen pictures of chickens before, but seeing one in real life, especially one so vibrant and full of personality, was something else entirely.

"Wow!" She exclaimed with shock, her curiosity piqued.

Onisa, with all the bravado of a child eager to impress, approached the bird.

"I'm gonna touch it," he declared, his hand outstretched.

"Onisa, be careful," Adaobi warned, her voice laced with both caution and amusement.

But Onisa wasn't listening. He moved closer, his fingers just inches from the cockerel's gleaming feathers when suddenly, the bird flapped its wings violently, letting out a loud squawk.

The reaction was immediate. Onisa yelped in fear and turned on his heel, running as fast as his legs could carry him. "It's going to kill me!" he screamed, his voice echoing through the compound as he fled.

Adaobi burst into laughter, doubling over as Onisa's cries filled the air. Their parents, who had been watching from a distance, couldn't help but chuckle as well.

"Onisa, it's just a chicken!" their father called out, trying to stifle his own laughter.

But Onisa wasn't having any of it. He kept running until he was safely behind their mother, peeking out from behind her skirt with wide, fearful eyes. "That thing is crazy!" he panted, glaring at the cockerel as if it were some kind of wild beast.

Adaobi finally caught her breath, still giggling. "You were so brave," she teased, nudging him lightly. "Maybe next time you'll think twice before trying to pet a chicken."

Onisa scowled, but there was a hint of a smile playing on his lips. "I wasn't scared," he muttered defensively. "It just… surprised me."

Their mother crouched down, pulling both into a hug. "This is just the beginning, my loves," she said softly. "There's so much more for you to discover here. You'll see, Nigeria has its own kind of magic."

As they pulled away from the embrace, Adaobi looked around, her eyes taking in the lush greenery and the vibrant life that surrounded them. She wasn't sure if she was ready for this new chapter, but for the first time, she felt a spark of excitement. There was a whole world here waiting to be explored, and she was determined to make the most of it, even if it meant facing a few more cockerels along the way.

Adaobi's high school dormitory life was a crucible of resilience. Every day, she grappled with the stark differences between the bustling streets of New York and the more subdued, unpredictable life in Nigeria. The convenience she once took for granted—the seamless access to Wi-Fi, the ease of ordering her favorite Chinese takeout, and the vibrant, never-sleeping atmosphere of the Bronx—was replaced by the erratic hum of generators and the spontaneous cheer of "Up NEPA!" whenever the power flickered back on.

Her first bout with malaria was a rude awakening, a stark reminder that she was no longer in the comfort of her familiar world.

"Ugh, I miss New York," Adaobi groaned one evening, swatting away a mosquito as she lay on her bunk, the heat pressing down like a heavy blanket.

"New York? Abeg, shift make I hear word," her bunkmate, Chioma, teased, her voice dripping with mockery. "Na for here you go learn survival, not for that oyibo place."

Adaobi rolled her eyes but couldn't help the small smile tugging at her lips. Chioma's sarcasm was starting to grow on her, a sign that she was slowly adjusting.

While her American accents and trendy clothes earned her admiration from some classmates, the dormitory bullies saw her as a target. They sought to remind her that no amount of American glamour could protect her from the harsh realities of Nigerian boarding school life.

"Look at her, Ms. America," sneered one of the older girls, Chinyere, as Adaobi walked past. "You think say we go worship you because you sabi speak through your nose?"

Adaobi bristled but kept walking, her heart pounding. "Just ignore them," she whispered to herself, clutching her books tighter. "It's just words."

Yet, amidst the challenges, there were moments that sparkled with unexpected joy. Like the day when, during a visit home, Adaobi finally understood one of her grandmother's long-told jokes—one wrapped in an adage she had heard countless times but never fully grasped.

They were sitting in the family's courtyard, the late afternoon sun casting a golden glow over everything. Her grandmother, with a teasing smile, said once again, "When the ear is told but does not hear, when the head is cut, the ear goes with it."

Adaobi paused, replaying the words in her mind, and then it suddenly clicked. Her eyes widened with realization, and laughter erupted from her.

"Oh! I get it now, Granny!" Adaobi exclaimed, her face lighting up as the meaning dawned on her. The proverb was about heeding advice—how the consequences of ignoring wisdom come too late.

Her grandmother, eyes twinkling, chuckled softly. "Ah, Adaobi, you are finally becoming one of us."

Adaobi grinned widely, feeling the warmth of her grandmother's words settle in her heart. It was as though, for the first time, she truly understood not only the humor but the deeper meaning behind the sayings that had shaped generations before her. In that moment, she felt an unspoken connection to her roots, to her family, and to the culture that had always been a part of her.

The first time she wore a traditional Igbo outfit, the vibrant colors and intricate designs made her feel connected to something deeper.

"Wow, Ada, you look like a real Igbo princess!" her cousin Nnenna admired, adjusting the headpiece, *gele* on Adaobi's head.

Adaobi beamed, twirling in front of the mirror. "I never thought I'd love this as much as I do."

As the months passed, something within Adaobi began to change. The foreignness of her new surroundings started to fade, and she found herself adjusting, even embracing, the rhythms of life in Nigeria. Her Igbo improved, no longer sounding so foreign on her tongue. The food, with its rich, spicy flavors, became something to savor rather than endure.

One afternoon, while enjoying a plate of jollof rice with her new friends, she found herself laughing freely.

"Who knew I'd actually like this stuff?" she said, popping another piece of plantain into her mouth.

Chioma grinned, "We knew it! You're becoming a true Naija babe."

Adaobi discovered the allure of Afrobeat music, its beats and rhythms speaking to a part of her that she hadn't known existed.

"Let's dance!" her friend Amaka shouted, grabbing her hand as Fela Kuti's "Water No Get Enemy" blasted from a nearby radio.

Adaobi hesitated for only a second before giving in, swaying her hips to the infectious rhythm. "This... this is actually fun!" she admitted, laughing.

Soon, she was dancing to Fela Kuti with the same passion she once reserved for Beyoncé. In time, Adaobi found herself not just surviving but thriving, bridging the worlds she came from and the ones she was growing to love.

By the time she was admitted to the University of Port Harcourt to study Microbiology, she had fully embraced her new environment. The culture shock that had once gripped her and her brother, Onisa, upon their arrival in Nigeria was now a distant memory. She was no longer the girl overwhelmed by the heat and the sea of black faces at the airport. Instead, Adaobi had become a bona fide Nigerian, deeply embedded in the fabric of the bustling campus life at UniPort.

However, one thing remained unchanged: her American accent. It was like a badge of honor she wore with pride, a remnant of her life in New York that she wasn't ready to let go of. And why would she? That accent, coupled with her trendy, head-turning garments, made her a force to be reckoned with on campus. She knew the power it held, and she wasn't afraid to wield it when necessary.

One afternoon, Adaobi strolled into a lecture hall, her head held high, wearing a pair of ripped jeans and a crop top that showed just enough skin to be fashionable without crossing any lines. Her Nike sneakers squeaked slightly against the tiled floor, drawing the attention of nearly everyone present. The buzz of conversation quieted as eyes followed her every move.

"Guy, see that babe," one of the boys whispered to his friend, nudging him with an elbow. "She too set, abeg. Na only her fit rock that kin cloth for this Naija and still get away with am."

His friend nodded, clearly in agreement. "And that accent, bro. She dey use am scatter everywhere."

Adaobi caught snippets of the conversation as she walked past but didn't acknowledge them. She was used to the stares, the whispers, the way people seemed to hang on her every word whenever she spoke in that unmistakable American twang. She reached her seat, settled in, and pulled out her notebook, ready to take on the day's lecture.

"Excuse me, is this seat taken?" a deep voice asked, breaking her concentration. Adaobi looked up to see a tall, muscular guy standing next to her, flashing a bright smile.

She smiled back, the corner of her lips curling mischievously.

"Depends," she replied, her accent unmistakably American. "What do you think?"

The guy chuckled, clearly taken by her charm. "I think I should take my chances," he said, sliding into the seat beside her.

Adaobi shook her head slightly, amused. "You're bold, I'll give you that."

"Name's Chidi," he introduced himself, extending his hand.

"Adaobi," she responded, shaking his hand with a firm grip. "Nice to meet you."

The lecture began, but Chidi couldn't seem to focus on anything other than Adaobi. Every time she raised her hand to ask a question, her American accent sliced through the room, commanding the attention of both the lecturer and the students. It was like she had a power switch, and she knew exactly when to flip it on.

After class, Chidi walked her out of the hall. "So, Adaobi, what part of the States are you from?" he asked, trying to keep the conversation light.

"Born and raised in the Bronx," she said, her voice filled with a sense of pride. "But I guess you could say I'm a little bit of everywhere now."

"I can see that," Chidi nodded. "You've got this whole mix of cultures going on. It's cool."

"Yeah, it has its perks," she replied, adjusting her backpack. "I can blend in when I want to or stand out when I need to."

Chidi laughed. "You definitely stand out. Not just because of the accent, but…everything. People notice you, and not just the guys."

Adaobi smiled, though a part of her wondered if people ever really saw beyond the accent and the clothes. "I guess that's one way to look at it," she said, her voice softening a bit. "But sometimes, it's nice to just…be."

Chidi seemed to catch the subtle change in her tone and quickly shifted gears. "Well, if you ever need someone to help you just 'be,' let me know," he offered, flashing another smile. "I'm pretty good at chilling."

Adaobi laughed, the sound light and genuine. "I'll keep that in mind, Chidi."

As they parted ways, Adaobi couldn't help but reflect on the conversation. She had become a bona fide Nigerian, yes, but the American in her would always be there, just beneath the surface, ready to resurface whenever she needed it. And perhaps that was her greatest strength, the ability to straddle two worlds and take the best from each.

Adaobi and Chidi's friendship blossomed naturally. What began as casual conversations after lectures quickly turned into study sessions, late-night phone calls, and eventually, something deeper. By her second year, they were inseparable, and it wasn't long before their friendship evolved into a full-blown relationship. Chidi was everything Adaobi could have asked for—caring, attentive, and always ready with a joke to brighten her day. He had a way of making her feel seen and valued in a way that others hadn't.

But there was something about Chidi that Adaobi couldn't quite put her finger on. He was always present, but sometimes, she caught the shadow of something darker lurking behind his eyes, a secret he kept hidden behind his easy smiles and gentle touch. Adaobi had asked him once, teasingly, about what he was hiding.

"Me? Hide something?" Chidi had said, raising an eyebrow playfully as he pulled her into a hug. "Come on, Ada. What you see is what you get."

She leaned back slightly, looking up into his eyes with a curious smile. "You sure about that? Sometimes I feel like there's more to you than you're letting on."

Chidi chuckled, brushing a loose strand of hair from her face.

"You're overthinking it, babe. I'm just a simple guy trying to keep up with his smart, beautiful girlfriend."

Adaobi giggled, the warmth of his words settling in her heart.

"Alright, I'll take your word for it," she said, though a small part of her remained unconvinced.

As their relationship deepened, Chidi became more than just a boyfriend; he was her confidant, her protector. They spent hours together, exploring the campus, studying late into the night, and even talking about the future. Adaobi felt safe with Chidi, and for the first time since she arrived in Nigeria, she felt like she had found someone who truly understood her.

But as her second year drew to a close, things started to change. Chidi became more distant, sometimes canceling their plans at the last minute or disappearing for days without a word. When he did show up, he was distracted, almost like his mind was somewhere else entirely.

One evening, as they sat under their favorite tree on campus, Adaobi couldn't hold back any longer.

"Chidi, what's going on?" she asked, her voice filled with concern. "You've been acting strange lately. Is everything okay?"

Chidi glanced at her, his usual playful demeanor replaced with something more somber. "I'm fine, Ada," he replied, though the lack of conviction in his voice was palpable. "Just a lot on my mind, you know? School, life, all that."

Adaobi wasn't convinced. She reached out, taking his hand in hers.

"You can talk to me about anything, you know that, right? I'm here for you."

Chidi looked down at their intertwined hands, his thumb brushing gently against her skin. "I know, Ada. And I appreciate it. I just... I need some time to sort things out. But I promise, it's nothing you need to worry about."

"Nothing I need to worry about?" Adaobi echoed; her voice tinged with frustration. "How can I not worry when you're shutting me out like this? We're supposed to be in this together, Chidi."

Chidi sighed, pulling her into a tight embrace. "I'm sorry, Ada. I didn't mean to make you feel that way. Just... trust me, okay? I'll make it right."

She buried her face in his chest, inhaling his familiar scent. "I do trust you," she whispered, though the unease in her heart was growing stronger with each passing day.

What Adaobi didn't know was that Chidi was living a double life. Beneath the surface of his charming, easy-going exterior, he was deeply involved in a secret world of violence and power. Chidi was not just a cult member; he was a Capone, a leader with a dark responsibility. He had managed to keep this part of his life hidden from Adaobi, protecting her from the dangers that lurked in the shadows of campus life.

But his secret life had caught up with him. Chidi had been given a task by his fellow cult members, one that made his blood run cold. He was to bring Adaobi to a party—a seemingly innocent event on the surface, but Chidi knew better. He knew what could happen to her, what was intended for her. The thought of Adaobi being hurt, defiled, in any way because of him, was more than he could bear.

One night, Chidi sat alone in his room, the weight of his decision pressing down on him. His phone buzzed with messages from Adaobi, but he couldn't bring himself to answer.

"Chidi, please talk to me," one of the messages read. "I'm worried about you."

Another buzz followed. "Did I do something wrong? Just tell me what's going on."

Chidi stared at the screen, his heart aching. He wanted to respond, to tell her everything, but he knew that doing so would put her in even greater danger. So instead, he made a decision that tore at his very soul. He would leave. It was the only way to protect Adaobi from the monsters he had associated with, even if it meant breaking her heart. He couldn't tell her the truth; it was too dangerous, too painful. So, without a word, he disappeared.

Adaobi was devastated. The next morning, she called him repeatedly, sent him countless messages, but there was no response. She went to his room, only to find it empty, his belongings gone. No one knew where he had gone or why he had left so suddenly. All she had were the memories they had shared, now tinged with a bitter sadness. The boy who had once made her feel so secure had vanished, leaving her to pick up the pieces of her shattered heart.

She sat on the edge of his bed, her fingers tracing the indentations on the pillow where he had slept. "Why, Chidi?" she whispered, tears streaming down her face. "Why did you leave me like this?"

Her phone remained silent; the last messages she had sent him were unanswered. The absence of closure gnawed at her, leaving her with a deep sense of loss and betrayal. Adaobi replayed their last conversation over and over in her mind, searching for clues, wondering if there had been signs, she had missed. Why had he vanished without a word?

The longer she waited, the more the weight of his silence pressed down on her, creating a hollow ache in her chest. It felt as if a part of her life had simply dissolved, leaving behind nothing but unanswered questions and a gaping void.

Little did she know, Chidi's departure was the ultimate act of love— a sacrifice to protect her from a fate she was unaware of. He had made the painful decision to disappear, knowing that staying in her life would only bring her pain. His own world was unraveling, and he couldn't bear the thought of dragging her into it.

But Adaobi, in her confusion and heartbreak, couldn't see the love in his silence. She only felt the sting of abandonment. The thought that someone she had once trusted could vanish so completely, without explanation, kept her up at night. All she wanted was an answer—any answer. Yet all she received was silence, a silence that deepened her wounds instead of healing them.

If only she had known the truth—that Chidi had loved her too much to let her get caught in the storm that was his life. But in her solitude, all she felt was the loss, unaware of the sacrifice behind it.

Adaobi was shattered by Chidi's sudden disappearance. The pain of losing him without any explanation plunged her into a deep depression.

Her once vibrant spirit dimmed, and the energetic, confident young woman who had captured the attention of so many on campus became a shadow of her former self. She withdrew from friends, stopped attending social gatherings, and even contemplated leaving school altogether. The university halls that had once felt like a new beginning now seemed like a cold, empty prison.

Days turned into weeks, and Adaobi's heartache only grew. She could barely focus on her studies, her grades slipping as she spiraled deeper into despair. The spark that had once made her so captivating was all but extinguished.

One evening, as she lay in her bed, staring at the ceiling with tear-stained eyes, Adaobi found herself praying. It wasn't something she had done in a long time, but at her lowest moment, she reached out for something—anything—that could pull her out of the darkness. She whispered, "God, if you're there... please, help me. I don't know what to do anymore."

The next day, feeling an inexplicable urge, she attended a Scripture Union meeting on campus. It was her first time stepping into such a gathering, and she was unsure of what to expect. The group was small, a mix of students who seemed genuinely kind and welcoming. As the meeting progressed, Adaobi found herself drawn to the words being spoken, the prayers, and the sense of peace that seemed to fill the room.

After the meeting, a girl approached her with a warm smile. "Hi, I'm Clara," she said, extending her hand. "I haven't seen you around before. Is this your first time?"

Adaobi nodded, a small smile tugging at her lips for the first time in weeks. "Yeah, it is. I'm Adaobi."

"Welcome, Adaobi," Clara said, her eyes shining with sincerity. "I'm really glad you came. I hope you'll join us again."

There was something about Clara's kindness that resonated with Adaobi. It was the first time in a long while that she felt someone genuinely cared. She started attending the meetings regularly, finding solace in the scriptures and the sense of community within the group. The more she immersed herself in her faith, the more she began to heal.

Adaobi's outward transformation reflected the changes happening within her. She began dressing more modestly, trading in her trendy garments for simpler, more subdued clothing. The once vibrant, bold Adaobi became quieter, more introspective. Her focus shifted entirely to her studies and her newfound faith. For a while, it seemed as though the light that had once made her shine had been dimmed forever.

But despite the drastic change, those who knew her well could see that Adaobi was slowly rebuilding herself. She was a shell of her former self, yes, but within that shell was the strength of someone who had survived heartbreak and found a new purpose. Through the support of the Scripture Union and her growing friendship with Clara, Adaobi began to piece her life back together, one prayer at a time.

By the time Adaobi reached her final year, the storm within her had started to calm. The deep wounds left by Chidi's sudden departure had slowly begun to heal, and the transformation she'd undergone in the Scripture Union had given her a new foundation. But as time passed, something within her began to stir—a desire to reconnect with the world she had once known.

It started subtly. Adaobi would linger a bit longer after SU meetings, chatting with friends about topics beyond scriptures and studies. She began accepting invitations to social events again, at first hesitantly, then with growing enthusiasm. The vibrant, confident girl who had once captivated everyone with her American accent and bold fashion choices was gradually reemerging, though with a softer, more introspective edge.

One afternoon, Clara noticed the change as they walked together across campus. Adaobi had just laughed at a joke Clara made—a real, genuine laugh that hadn't been heard in a long time.

"It's good to see you smile like that again, Adaobi," Clara said, nudging her playfully.

Adaobi smiled, a little shy. "I guess... I'm starting to feel more like myself again."

"That's the Adaobi I remember," Clara said warmly. "You know, it's okay to let yourself be happy again. It's what he would have wanted for you."

Adaobi paused, looking at Clara with a mixture of surprise and gratitude. "You think so?"

Clara nodded. "I know so. We've all seen how strong you've become. But it's okay to let that strength show in your joy, too."

Adaobi took a deep breath, feeling the truth in Clara's words.

"Maybe you're right. I've spent so long trying to bury everything that happened... maybe it's time to let go."

From that day forward, Adaobi began to open up more, allowing herself to enjoy the company of others and embrace the joy that had once been such a natural part of her. The quiet strength she had cultivated over the years blended with the vibrant spirit she had always carried within her, creating a new version of herself—one that was both resilient and full of life.

As Adaobi's graduation loomed closer, the suitors began to circle.

She was no longer the broken girl who had hidden herself away in the pages of scripture and solitude. The vibrancy she had once been known for had returned, but it was now tempered with wisdom and caution. The pain of her past, especially the betrayal she felt from Chidi's sudden disappearance, had made her more guarded, and she became meticulous in assessing anyone who tried to win her heart.

It was during this time that Afam came into the picture. Freshly returned from the USA, he had all the trappings of a man who had seen the world—smooth in his mannerisms, polished in his speech, and dressed in the kind of understated style that screamed affluence without the need for gaudy displays. He was, by all accounts, a catch.

Their first date was set up at a quaint restaurant just off campus, a place known for its quiet corners and candle-lit tables. Afam had chosen well.

As they settled into their seats, Adaobi could feel the weight of his gaze on her. She was used to being admired, but there was something about Afam's intensity that made her uneasy, though she couldn't quite place why.

"So, Adaobi," Afam began with a smile that was just a little too confident.

"What do you miss most about the States?"

She chuckled lightly, playing along. "The food, definitely. And the weather. It's not as unpredictable as here."

Afam nodded, seemingly pleased with her answer. "Yeah, I miss that too. But there's something about home, right? Even with all the chaos, it's where we truly belong."

As they spoke, Afam reached into his pocket and pulled out a pack of Big Red chewing gum. He tore open the pack and unwrapped a single piece, holding it out to her.

"Want some?" he offered; his voice smooth.

"Sure, thanks," Adaobi replied, accepting the gum. She was about to make a joke about how Americans always seemed to have gum on them, but Afam's next move stopped her short. Instead of handing her the pack, he tucked it back into his pocket.

The conversation flowed, though Adaobi found herself distracted by Afam's curious habit. Every so often, he would reach into his pocket, pull out the pack, and offer her another piece, always unwrapping it and handing it to her directly. By the third time, Adaobi couldn't help but feel a twinge of irritation.

Was he rationing his gum? Or worse, was he testing her?

After the fourth piece was offered, Adaobi raised an eyebrow, her patience thinning. "Afam," she said, her tone light but edged with something sharper, "you know, it's okay to just give me the whole pack. I won't bite."

Afam looked momentarily taken aback, then laughed, though the sound didn't quite reach his eyes. "Oh, come on, Adaobi. It's just gum. What's the big deal?"

She leaned back in her chair, her gaze steady. "It's not the gum, Afam. It's the idea of holding back when you don't need to. If we're going to get to know each other, I'd prefer it if we didn't start with half measures."

The atmosphere at the table shifted, the easy banter turning into something more guarded. Afam smiled, but it was tighter now, and he reluctantly pulled out a full pack of gum, handing it to her without another word.

Adaobi accepted it with a polite nod, but the damage was done. Throughout the rest of the evening, she found herself more and more detached, mentally checking out of the date as Afam continued talking, seemingly oblivious to the shift in her demeanor.

As they parted ways, Afam tried to set up a second date, but Adaobi was noncommittal. "Let's see," she said with a smile that didn't reach her eyes, leaving him with a vague promise to catch up later.

Walking back to her dorm, Adaobi mulled over the evening. It wasn't just the gum—it was the principle. The tiny, seemingly insignificant gestures spoke volumes to her now. After what she had gone through with Chidi, she had learned to read between the lines, to pick up on the subtle cues that others might overlook. Afam's behavior, his reluctance to give fully and his tendency to hold back, was a red flag she couldn't ignore.

Adaobi knew she had every right to be picky. She deserved someone who wouldn't make her feel like she had to earn every little piece of affection, someone who would give without hesitation. As she slipped the pack of Big Red into her bag, she smiled to herself, knowing that she was no longer the girl who would settle for less. The right person would come along when the time was right, and until then, she was perfectly content to wait.

Following her return to the USA soon after completing her university studies in Nigeria brought about a period of adjustment for Adaobi. Moving back to the country where she had spent her earlier years, she faced the challenge of reacclimating to a familiar yet changed environment. The shift was more pronounced because her family had relocated to White Plains, a quieter and more suburban area compared to the bustling Bronx where she had grown up.

She also couldn't help but feel a sense of loss. In Nigeria, she had been the center of attention—her American accent and trendy outfits had set her apart in a way that made her feel unique and admired. But back in the States, it was a different story.

Here, she blended in more than she stood out. The vibrancy of her fashion choices and the way she carried herself no longer drew the same level of attention. Instead, she found herself grappling with a new reality—one where her opportunities seemed more limited as a Black woman in America. The confidence she had built up during her time in Nigeria now felt shaken, and the weight of societal expectations and barriers pressed down on her.

As she continued the daunting task of job hunting, the process was also made more challenging by the fact that many of her old friends had moved on, leaving her with a sense of isolation in a place that no longer felt entirely like home.

Adaobi was at the dining table, laptop open, with a list of job applications she'd been working on. The house was quiet, except for the faint hum of the refrigerator. Her phone rang, interrupting her concentration. It was her mother calling from upstairs.

"Hi, Mom," Adaobi answered, trying to sound upbeat.

"Hello, Adaobi," her mother replied warmly. "How are you doing? Settling in alright?"

"Yeah, I'm getting there," Adaobi said, pushing aside the laptop. "Just working on some job applications."

There was a brief pause before her mother spoke again. "That's good. I'm proud of you for being so focused. But I wanted to talk about something else too."

Adaobi sighed internally, already sensing where this conversation was heading. "Sure, Mom. What's up?"

"You know, Adaobi, it's been a week since you've been back, and I can't help but think about your future," her mother began, her tone gentle but firm. "You've done so well in school, and I know you'll find a good job soon. But what about starting a family?"

"Mom, we've talked about this," Adaobi replied, trying to keep her voice calm. "I'm just getting back on my feet here. I want to focus on my career first."

"I understand that." her mother said, her voice softening. "But it's important to think about these things now. You know how our culture is—finding the right person takes time. And I just want to see you happy, with someone who understands our values."

Adaobi leaned back in her chair, feeling the familiar weight of expectation.

"I know you mean well, Mom, but I don't want to rush into anything. I'll meet someone when the time is right."

Her mother sighed. "I'm not asking you to rush, Adaobi. I just want you to keep your heart open, especially to someone who shares our background. You know how much it would mean to your father and me."

Adaobi felt a pang of guilt but remained firm. "I get it, Mom. I really do. But can we not make this a regular thing? I have enough on my plate right now."

Her mother chuckled lightly. "Alright, alright. I won't push. But just promise me you'll think about it."

Adaobi smiled, relieved that her mother wasn't pressing the issue further. "I will, Mom. I promise. But for now, let me focus on getting a job, okay?"

"Okay, my dear," her mother said, her tone affectionate. "Take your time, but remember, we're here to support you in every way. I just want what's best for you."

"I know, Mom," Adaobi replied, feeling a mix of gratitude and frustration. "Thanks for understanding."

"Anytime, Adaobi," her mother said warmly. "Now, don't stay up too late. You need your rest."

Adaobi laughed. "I won't, Mom. Goodnight."

"Goodnight, my dear," her mother replied before ending the call.

Adaobi set her phone down and sighed, feeling both comforted by her mother's care and slightly overwhelmed by her expectations. She glanced back at her laptop, determined to take things one step at a time.

Adaobi had been job hunting for months, and when she finally received an offer from Kings County Hospital Center in Brooklyn, it felt like a long-awaited breakthrough. The job in the hospital laboratory was a solid step forward, a chance to finally settle into her life in the USA.

The first few weeks were a blur of learning new protocols, getting to know her colleagues, and adjusting to the fast pace of life in New York. It didn't take long for Adaobi to realize that driving in the city was a nightmare. The traffic was relentless, and finding parking was almost impossible. So, she quickly adapted to using the trains, which were more reliable and far less stressful.

At the hospital, she found herself surrounded by a diverse group of coworkers, each bringing their unique perspectives to the team. Adaobi was quick to make friends, bonding over shared lunch breaks and late-night shifts. There was Maria, who always had the best snack recommendations, and Jared, who shared Adaobi's love for Nollywood movies.

One afternoon, during a rare quiet moment in the lab, Maria leaned over to Adaobi with a grin.

"So, Adaobi, any special someone in your life? You're always so mysterious about it."

Adaobi chuckled, shaking her head. "No, no one special. I've just been focusing on work and settling in."

Maria raised an eyebrow. "Girl, you've been here for years! You deserve to have some fun too, you know."

"I know, I know," Adaobi replied with a sigh. "But honestly, it's been tough. I haven't really connected with anyone on that level."

Jared, who had been listening in, chimed in with a smirk. "Maybe you're just too picky, Adaobi."

"Or maybe I just haven't found the right person," Adaobi countered, though her smile didn't quite reach her eyes.

As much as she enjoyed her work and the friendships she had made, there was a lingering sense of loneliness that Adaobi couldn't shake. Despite her best efforts, her romantic life remained stagnant, and she often found herself wondering if she was missing out on something important.

Four years passed in a blur of work, occasional outings with friends, and countless train rides across the city. One evening, Adaobi decided to treat herself to a night out and bought a ticket to see *The Lion King* on Broadway. It was a show she had always wanted to see, and she figured it would be a nice way to unwind.

As the final curtain fell and the audience erupted into applause, Adaobi felt a sense of contentment. She gathered her things and made her way out of the theater, blending into the crowd of excited theatergoers spilling onto the street.

Just as she was about to head toward the subway, she heard a familiar voice call out, "Adaobi?"

She turned, scanning the crowd, and there she was—Clara. Clara's smile was as bright as ever, her eyes lighting up with recognition.

"Clara?" Adaobi exclaimed, her heart skipping a beat. "Is that really you?"

"It's me!" Clara replied, laughing as she pushed through the crowd to get to Adaobi. "I can't believe it! How long has it been?"

"Too long!" Adaobi said as they embraced, the warmth of the hug making the years apart melt away. "I've missed you! What are you doing here?"

"I could ask you the same thing!" Clara said, her eyes wide with excitement. "I have been here for almost 2 years. I've been meaning to reach out, but life got in the way. And now look at us, running into each other like this!"

"It's fate," Adaobi said with a grin. "We've got so much to catch up on."

As Adaobi and Clara embraced outside the theater, Clara stepped back, revealing the man standing beside her.

"Adaobi, this is my husband, Emeka," Clara introduced with a proud smile.

Adaobi's eyes widened in surprise.

"Emeka! Wow, it's so great to finally meet you! Clara told me so much about you back then."

Emeka grinned and extended his hand. "It's a pleasure to meet you, Adaobi. Clara's talked about you often. I feel like I already know you."

Adaobi shook his hand warmly. "Likewise! I'm sorry I couldn't make it to your wedding. Life was so hectic at the time, and I had to return here."

Clara waved her hand dismissively. "Oh, don't worry about it! I know you were swamped. Besides, we're here now, and that's what matters."

Adaobi nodded, though she felt a small pang of regret for missing such an important moment in her friend's life. She remembered their story and how Clara had excitedly told her, "Adaobi, if he ever proposes, I'll say yes in a heartbeat!"

And she did. Clara had called Adaobi shortly after the proposal, ecstatic and giddy, to share the good news. Now, seeing them together, Adaobi could see just how right they were for each other.

Emeka had his arm around Clara, and the way they looked at each other spoke volumes about the happiness they had found together.

"So, you've been in the States for almost two years now?" Adaobi asked as they started walking toward a nearby café.

"Yes! I moved here to be with Emeka after we got married," Clara explained, her voice full of contentment. "It's been an adjustment, but I couldn't be happier. We're really enjoying life together."

"That's wonderful," Adaobi said, genuinely pleased for her friend. "You two look so happy. I'm really glad things have worked out so well."

"We are happy," Clara replied, squeezing Emeka's hand. "It hasn't always been easy, but we've grown a lot together. How about you, Adaobi? How's everything been on your end?"

Adaobi hesitated for a moment, not wanting to dampen the mood with her own challenges. "It's been... a journey," she finally said with a small smile. "I've been working at a hospital lab in Brooklyn, and I've made some great friends. But, you know, still trying to figure out the whole romance thing."

Clara nodded sympathetically "I get it. But don't worry, Adaobi. Things have a way of working out when you least expect them."

Emeka chimed in, "You're a strong, amazing woman, Adaobi. The right person will come along when the time is right."

Adaobi smiled, feeling a bit more hopeful. "Thanks, Emeka. I appreciate that."

As they settled into the cozy café, Adaobi, Clara and Emeka immediately felt the warm, inviting ambiance wrap around them. The space was intimate, with soft lighting casting a golden glow over rustic wooden tables and plush, cushioned chairs. The air was scented with freshly ground coffee and baked pastries, a comforting blend that made the outside world feel far away.

Tucked into a corner by the window, their table was surrounded by tall bookshelves filled with worn, well-loved novels, adding to the café's charm. Potted plants and creeping vines hung from shelves and windowsills, giving the room a soft, natural touch. The crackle of a small fireplace in the corner added a comforting warmth to the cool afternoon, and the gentle hum of quiet conversations and soft jazz playing in the background made it the perfect refuge from the hustle and bustle of the city outside.

They sank into their chairs, the cushions molding to their forms, as the barista, with a warm smile, brought over their steaming cups of coffee. It was the kind of place where time seemed to slow down, and the cozy atmosphere made it easy to relax and lose themselves in conversation.

The three of them continued to chat, sharing stories and laughter.

Adaobi couldn't help but feel grateful for this unexpected reunion. Seeing Clara so happy with Emeka gave her hope that maybe, just maybe, her own path would lead to a happiness of her own someday.

Adaobi's friends often encouraged her to be open to new connections, but after several unsuccessful attempts, she had grown cautious. So, when Eze, a friend of a friend, suggested she meet his buddy Okechukwu, she was hesitant.

"Come on, Adaobi," Eze had urged over the phone. "Okechukwu is a good guy—smart, successful, and I think you two would really hit it off. At least give it a chance."

"I don't know, Eze," Adaobi had replied, uncertainty clear in her voice. "I'm not sure I'm ready to start something new."

"Just exchange numbers with him, and if it doesn't work out, no pressure," Eze had insisted.

After a moment's pause, Adaobi agreed. "Alright, fine. I'll give it a shot."

The first few phone calls with Okechukwu were surprisingly pleasant. His deep, resonant voice was comforting, and they found themselves laughing and talking about a range of topics. Adaobi began to think that maybe, just maybe, this could turn into something.

But then, Okechukwu emailed her some pictures of himself. Adaobi opened the email with a mix of curiosity and apprehension. As she clicked through the images, her excitement started to wane. The photos seemed overly posed, as if he were trying too hard to project a certain image.

He's definitely confident, she thought to herself, but is this what I'm looking for?

Still, she decided to meet him in person, hoping that the chemistry they had over the phone might translate better face-to-face. Okechukwu was flying into New York for a business trip, and they arranged to meet at the airport.

The day of their meeting, Adaobi arrived at the airport early, her heart pounding with anticipation. She spotted him almost immediately as he emerged from the arrivals gate. But as she watched him push his luggage trolley, something felt, off.

Okechukwu moved with a deliberate swagger, carefully maneuvering his trolley, which was piled high with expensive-looking luggage. Adaobi couldn't help but notice how meticulously he handled his bags.

Who brings so much luggage for a few days? She wondered.

As Okechukwu approached, he greeted her with a broad smile.

"Adaobi! It's so good to finally meet you in person."

"Hi, Okechukwu," Adaobi replied, forcing a smile because she was oddly not taken by him. "It's nice to meet you too."

They made their way to his car, where Okechukwu began to unload his bags with exaggerated care. Adaobi's eyes widened as she saw just how many there were.

"Wow, you brought a lot of stuff," she remarked, trying to keep her tone neutral.

Okechukwu chuckled, brushing off her comment. "Ah, you know how it is. I like to be prepared for any occasion."

As they drove to his hotel, Okechukwu handed her a small gift bag. "I got you something," he said with a wink.

Adaobi opened the bag to find a 50 ml bottle of Estée Lauder perfume. She thanked him politely, but the gesture felt underwhelming, especially when she noticed the high-end Creed cologne he was wearing.

So much for thoughtfulness, she mused inwardly.

During his visit, Okechukwu's behavior only reinforced Adaobi's growing unease. He seemed overly concerned with his appearance, constantly adjusting his clothes and checking his reflection in every available surface. His conversations often circled back to his possessions, his watch collection, his designer suits, his luxury colognes.

On the third day of his stay, they sat down for lunch at a trendy café. Adaobi had been quiet, her mind racing as she tried to make sense of her feelings.

Okechukwu noticed her silence. "You've been awfully quiet today, Adaobi. Is everything okay?"

Adaobi looked up, meeting his gaze. "Honestly, Okechukwu, I'm just trying to figure out if we're really on the same page."

Okechukwu frowned, genuinely confused. "What do you mean?"

She took a deep breath. "You're clearly very successful and confident, but I feel like you're more interested in appearances and material things than in getting to know me or in a genuine connection."

He blinked, taken aback. "Adaobi, I didn't mean to give that impression. I thought you'd appreciate someone who takes care of himself."

"It's not about that," she said softly. "It's just… I'm looking for something more meaningful, something real. And I don't think we're looking for the same things."

Okechukwu nodded slowly, a look of understanding and disappointment crossing his face. "I see. I guess I was trying too hard to impress you."

Adaobi offered a small, sympathetic smile. "I appreciate the effort, Okechukwu, but I think we're just different people with different priorities."

The rest of the lunch was cordial but subdued. As they said their goodbyes, Adaobi felt a sense of relief mixed with regret. She knew she had made the right decision, but it was still hard to walk away from what might have been.

Later that evening, as she reflected on the experience, Adaobi realized that she needed to stay true to herself and what she wanted in a relationship. And she knew that eventually, she would find someone who valued the same things she did.

IKUNNU

Clara walked down the corridor of Hostel C, her sandals tapping softly against the concrete floor as the afternoon sun blazed through the narrow windows. She counted the room numbers on the peeling doors until she came to 217. *This has to be it,* she thought, pausing outside Stella's room.

The heat of the UniPort campus was relentless, and sweat clung to her forehead, making her feel sticky and uncomfortable. She shifted the borrowed textbook from one hand to the other, using it to fan herself while glancing down the hallway.

Please let her be in, Clara thought. The idea of walking all the way back to her own room in the scorching sun without returning the book made her sigh. She knocked on the door, the metal rattling slightly as her knuckles made contact, hoping to retreat soon to the cooler confines of her room where a cold bottle of Fanta waited for her.

As she knocked on the door, she could hear the faint sound of music playing inside.

The door opened to reveal Stella, her cheerful face lighting up.

"Clara! You made it! Come on in, girl."

Clara stepped inside, smiling at her friend. Stella was as vibrant as ever, her energy filling the room. As Clara moved further in, her gaze landed on Ikunnu, who was lounging on her bed, flipping through a fashion magazine.

"Oh, it's you, Clara!" Ikunnu said, looking up with a smile. She was dressed in a colorful Ankara jumpsuit that demanded attention.

"Come to return a book?"

Clara nodded, holding up the novel. "Yep, I figured I should get it back to you, Stella, before the weekend rush starts."

Stella grinned, reaching out to take the book. "Thanks! I've been dying to dive into this one."

As Clara handed over the book, her eyes were drawn to a photograph on a small pedestal near Ikunnu's bed. She froze, the familiar face in the picture sending a jolt through her.

"That's… that's my uncle!" Clara exclaimed, unable to hide her shock.

Ikunnu, who had been lost in her magazine, looked up sharply.

"What do you mean, your uncle? That's my father."

Stella, sensing the tension, looked back and forth between the two of them, her eyes widening. "Wait, what?"

Clara stared at the photograph, her mind racing. "No, that's definitely my uncle," she insisted, her voice shaking slightly. "He… he's the one who…" She trailed off, not wanting to dredge up painful memories in front of Ikunnu and Stella.

Ikunnu's brow furrowed as she processed this. "If that's your uncle and my father, then… does that make us… cousins?"

The room was thick with silence, the weight of the revelation sinking in.

Stella was the first to speak, her voice full of amazement. "No way! Are you two related? That's insane!"

Ikunnu blinked a few times, then burst out laughing. "Well, damn! Who would've thought? This world is too small, I swear."

Clara managed to smile, her heart still pounding. "Yeah, it really is."

From that moment on, Clara and Ikunnu's relationship shifted.

Despite the complicated history between their parents, Clara chose not to let it come between them. They were family, after all, and she wasn't about to let old wounds dictate their future.

As the weeks passed, Clara found herself spending more time with Ikunnu and Stella. She got to know Ikunnu better, discovering just how different they were. Ikunnu was the definition of flamboyance. After every summer holiday, she would return to campus with tales of her travels to Spain, London, or the USA.

"I was in London for two weeks," Ikunnu would boast, flipping her braided hair over her shoulder. "The shopping there is to die for! You wouldn't believe the deals I got."

Stella would always be the first to chime in, wide-eyed. "London? That's amazing! What did you buy?"

Clara, who knew the campus gossip all too well, kept her thoughts to herself. She'd heard the whispers—how Ikunnu never showed any pictures of her trips, how people speculated that she just went to Aba to buy grade A *"Okirika"*, secondhand clothes instead.

"She only has the clothes to prove it," one of their classmates had once said, smirking. "But where's the evidence of all these travels?"

Then there was an infamous incident with Ikunnu's mother. Clara still remembered how it had gone down. Ikunnu's mother had come to visit her on campus, arriving by bus and then hitching a ride on a bike. She'd brought with her a simple, traditional gift: a basket of "ukwa," the breadfruit delicacy.

Ikunnu had been mortified. "I almost died of embarrassment, Clara!" she had exclaimed later, her face flushed with indignation. Stella had been there too, trying—and failing—to stifle her giggles.

"Of all things to bring, she had to bring '*ukwa,*" Ikunnu continued, throwing her hands up in exasperation. "And the way she showed up, like she'd never heard of a car before."

Clara had just smiled, shaking her head. "She's your mother, Ikunnu. She probably thought you'd appreciate the effort."

Stella, still laughing, had added, "At least it wasn't yam or something. You could have been stuck with a sack of that."

Ikunnu had huffed, but the tension soon melted into laughter. That was just Ikunnu—bold, brash, and unafraid to speak her mind, even if it meant exaggerating the truth a little.

And Clara? She wouldn't have had her cousin any other way.

Ikunnu was also a force of nature, always buzzing with energy and dragging Clara into her whirlwind of activities. But after Ifeyinwa convinced Clara to start attending SU meetings, Clara felt a new sense of peace and wanted to share it with her cousin.

One afternoon, after a particularly uplifting SU meeting, Clara found herself sitting with Ikunnu in the courtyard, the sun casting long shadows across the grass.

"Ikunnu, you should really come to one of the SU meetings," Clara said, her voice gentle but insistent. "It's not what you think. It's… peaceful. And the fellowship, it's something special."

Ikunnu, who had been absentmindedly twirling a strand of her hair, shot her a playful grin. "Peaceful? Clara, you know I live for excitement, not sitting around praying all day. Besides, if I start going to SU meetings, who's going to keep the campus parties alive?"

Clara chuckled. "You could do both, you know. Balance is key."

But Ikunnu wasn't swayed. "Tell you what, I'll make you a deal. You come to one of the weekend parties with me, and I'll consider going to SU."

Clara smiled, shaking her head. "Nice try, but I think I'll stick with SU. You'll be surprised how much you might like it."

Ikunnu waved her off, though there was no real heat in her dismissal. "You're lucky you're my cousin, or I'd keep pestering you until you agreed to come."

Despite her reluctance to attend the official SU meetings, something about the quiet prayers and close-knit group of Clara's friends intrigued Ikunnu. On more than one occasion, she found herself joining in on their impromptu prayer sessions in their dorm rooms. What started as curiosity gradually turned into something more meaningful.

Even Ifeyinwa, Chinelo, and Adaobi, who had initially been unsure about Ikunnu's loud personality, began to warm to her. In those moments of prayer, Ikunnu's bravado softened, and she allowed herself to be vulnerable, connecting with Clara's inner circle in a way she hadn't expected.

"Who would have thought?" Ifeyinwa mused one evening after a prayer session, glancing at Ikunnu with a smile. "You're almost one of us now."

Ikunnu rolled her eyes, though the corners of her mouth lifted into a grin. "Don't get too excited. I'm still the life of the party around here. But… you lot aren't so bad either."

Clara exchanged a knowing look with Ifeyinwa and the others. Beneath the flashy exterior, they'd come to see the heart of gold Ikunnu tried so hard to hide. And while she might never be a regular at the SU meetings, she had become an integral part of their circle in her own unique way.

As graduation loomed, the usual buzz of excitement and anxiety filled the campus. Students were either neck-deep in final projects or dreaming of what lay beyond the university gates. But for Ikunnu, a different kind of storm was brewing inside her.

One evening, as the sun dipped low and cast a golden hue across the campus, Ikunnu asked Clara to take a walk with her.

They strolled in silence for a while, the air thick with unspoken words. Finally, Ikunnu stopped near a secluded bench, away from the usual hustle of students. She sat down, her usual confidence replaced with a nervous energy that Clara had never seen before.

"Clara," Ikunnu began, her voice unsteady, "I need to tell you something. But I don't even know where to start."

Clara, sensing the gravity of the moment, sat beside her cousin, placing a reassuring hand on her knee. "Whatever it is, you can tell me, Ikunnu. I'm here for you."

Ikunnu took a deep breath, her eyes misting over. "I'm pregnant."

Clara's breath caught in her throat. "Pregnant? Ikunnu, how—"

"It's Chief Idowu," Ikunnu cut in, her voice breaking. "He's the father and we just started dating 3 months ago."

Clara's eyes widened in shock. She knew about Ikunnu's new sugar daddy, Chief Idowu, a wealthy Yoruba man who already had two wives. But hearing it now, in this context, was like a punch to the gut.

"What are you going to do?" Clara asked softly, her concern etched on her face.

Ikunnu shook her head, tears welling up in her eyes. "I don't know, Clara. I really don't. Chief Idowu… he wants me to be his third wife. He's ready to take responsibility. But my father… oh God, my father will kill me if he finds out. He's so strict, Clara. He'll disown me if I have a baby out of wedlock, let alone marry a man with two wives already!"

For the first time, Clara saw Ikunnu without her usual bravado. Her cousin, who was always so bold and fearless, was now trembling with fear and uncertainty. Clara's heart ached for her.

"Have you told Chief Idowu about your father?" Clara asked, her voice gentle.

Ikunnu nodded, wiping away a tear that had escaped down her cheek. "He understands, but he says it's my decision to make. He's not pressuring me, but Clara… I'm scared. What if my father finds out? What if he disowns me? I'll have nowhere to go."

Clara took Ikunnu's hands in hers, squeezing them tightly. "You're not alone, Ikunnu. Whatever you decide, we'll figure it out together. You have us—me, Ifeyinwa, Adaobi, Chinelo. We're your family too."

Ikunnu looked at Clara, her eyes brimming with a mix of fear and gratitude. "I don't know what to do, Clara. I've never felt this lost before."

Clara pulled her cousin into a tight embrace. "We'll get through this, Ikunnu. I promise. You don't have to face this alone."

For the first time in a long while, Ikunnu allowed herself to cry, to let out all the fear and anxiety that had been building inside her. And in that moment, surrounded by the quiet of the evening and the comforting presence of her cousin, she felt a glimmer of hope that maybe, just maybe, everything would be okay.

Clara held Ikunnu close, her mind racing with questions. After a moment, she gently pulled back and gazed into Ikunnu's tear-filled eyes.

"Have you told your mother yet?" Clara asked softly, hoping for a sliver of good news.

Ikunnu shook her head, wiping her eyes with the back of her hand.

"No, not yet. My mother… she won't be a problem. She's always been more understanding, but I just… I haven't found the courage to tell her. I know she'll worry, but it's my father I'm most afraid of."

Clara nodded, understanding the weight of Ikunnu's fears. "Maybe telling your mother first could help. She might be able to soften the blow when the time comes to tell your father."

Ikunnu sighed deeply, her shoulders sagging under the burden of it all. "Maybe. But I just don't know how to even start that conversation. Everything feels so overwhelming."

Clara squeezed her cousin's hand again, offering a small smile.

"We'll figure it out together, Ikunnu. When you're ready and if you want me to come along, we can talk to your mother. I'm sure she'll understand, and she'll help you through this."

Ikunnu nodded, the fear still lingering in her eyes, but a bit of the weight seemed to lift as she leaned on Clara's unwavering support.

When Ikunnu returned home, she sat on the edge of her bed, her heart heavy with the decision she knew she had to make. For days, she had rehearsed the conversation in her mind, but now that the moment had come, she felt the weight of it pressing down on her.

Finally, she stood, smoothing her dress nervously, and made her way to the kitchen, where her mother was peeling yams.

Her mother looked up, sensing something was amiss. "What is it, my dear? You've been so quiet lately. Is everything okay?" she asked, her voice full of concern.

Ikunnu took a deep breath, her words trembling as she spoke. "Mama, I'm pregnant."

The knife in her mother's hand froze mid-air, her eyes locking onto Ikunnu's with a mix of shock and worry. "Pregnant? Ikunnu, whose child, is it? What's going on?" she asked, her voice edged with fear.

"It's Chief Idowu's," Ikunnu replied, her voice barely above a whisper. "He wants to take responsibility, Mama. He wants to marry me." The words hung in the air, heavy with implications.

"Chief Idowu?" her mother repeated, trying to process the revelation. "The one with all the businesses in Abuja? But… Ikunnu, isn't he already married?"

Ikunnu nodded, her gaze dropping to the floor. "Yes, Mama. He has two wives already. His first wife is in Lagos, and the second one is in Calabar. But he says they don't see each other often. He's promised to set me up in Abuja, in a house of my own. There won't be any need for competition or fighting between us."

Her mother sighed deeply, placing the yam and knife down on the table. She looked at her daughter, seeing the mix of fear and determination in her eyes. "Third wife… Ikunnu, are you sure this is the life you want? Marriage to a man who already has two other wives. What about your happiness, your future?"

Ikunnu swallowed hard, searching for the right words. "Mama, I've thought about it long and hard. Chief Idowu is kind, and he's offered me a life I could only dream of. You know how we've struggled, how hard it's been to make ends meet. This could change everything, not just for me but for all of us. I've always wanted more... a better life, a chance to rise above our circumstances."

Her mother studied her daughter's face, the lines of worry deepening on her own. "I know you, Ikunnu. You've always had big dreams, always reached for more. But being a third wife... it's not an easy path. There will be challenges, loneliness even. Affluence and power can be enticing, but they can also come with their own set of troubles."

Ikunnu nodded, tears welling in her eyes. "I know, Mama. But Chief Idowu has promised to take care of me. I won't be like the other wives, hidden away. He said he'll give me my own space, my own life in Abuja. I'll be independent, Mama. And with his connections and influence, I could even start a business, build something of my own."

Her mother sighed, her mind turning to Ikunnu's father. "And what about your father? You know how he is... proud, stubborn. This news will be hard for him to swallow."

"I know, Mama," Ikunnu replied softly. "But Chief Idowu has also offered to help us. He said he'll buy Papa a car, and even rebuild our home. Maybe if Papa sees how serious Chief is about taking care of us, he won't be so angry. Maybe he'll understand that this is a good opportunity for all of us."

There was a long silence as her mother considered everything she said, prior to finally nodding, though the worry in her eyes remained.

"Ikunnu, I can see that your mind is made up. You've always been a strong-willed girl, and I know you'll do what you think is best. If this is truly what you want, then you have my blessing. But remember, wealth and status can change a person. Don't lose yourself in all of this. Stay true to who you are, no matter what."

Tears finally spilled down Ikunnu's cheeks as she reached out to grasp her mother's hand. "Thank you, Mama. I promise I won't forget who I am. I just want to make things better for all of us."

Her mother squeezed her hand gently, offering a small, reassuring smile. "Then go, my daughter. Walk your path with wisdom and grace. And may it bring you the happiness you seek."

The sun cast long shadows across the compound as the drumming reached a crescendo, announcing the arrival of Chief Idowu's impressive convoy a few weeks later. A sleek black Mercedes G-Wagon led the way, its polished exterior reflecting the vibrant colors of the gathered crowd. Behind it, a procession of luxury vehicles followed, each one a testament to the Chief's wealth and status.

As the convoy came to a stop, the doors of the G-Wagon opened, and Chief Idowu stepped out, his presence commanding immediate attention. He was dressed in a deep purple agbada, the fabric rich and flowing, adorned with gold embroidery that caught the light. His entourage quickly surrounded him, carrying gifts and crates of drinks. Among them was a brand new 2015 black Toyota Sienna, a gift for Ikunnu's father, which was ceremoniously presented at the entrance of the compound.

The crowd buzzed with excitement as Chief Idowu approached Ikunnu's father, who stood waiting with a mix of curiosity and caution. His white kaftan contrasted sharply with the dark vehicle, a symbol of the contrast between his modest life and the opulence that Chief Idowu represented.

"Mr. Okeke, it is an honor to be here today," Chief Idowu began, his voice strong and clear. He gestured towards the Toyota Sienna. "This is a token of my respect and admiration for you, sir. I come today not just to greet you but to formally introduce myself in the spirit of tradition. This is the knocking ceremony, where I seek your blessing to unite our families through marriage."

Mr. Okeke's eyes widened slightly at the sight of the car, but he quickly composed himself. "Chief Idowu, your generosity is truly humbling," he replied, shaking Chief Idowu's hand firmly. "Please, come inside so we may continue with the proceedings."

Inside, the living room was filled with family members and close friends, all eager to witness the ceremony. The talking drum continued to play softly in the background, creating a rhythmic heartbeat that underscored the importance of the occasion.

As the drinks were poured and the formalities began, Ikunnu was called into the room. The murmurs from the gathered guests hushed as she made her entrance, moving gracefully with her head slightly bowed, a symbol of respect for the elders seated in a semi-circle. She walked with poise, her every step deliberate, as the weight of tradition pressed on her shoulders. In her hands, she carried an ornately decorated tray, shimmering with gold accents and intricate carvings, its beauty a reflection of the significance of the occasion.

On the tray rested a small calabash gourd filled with freshly tapped palm-wine, its earthy aroma mingling with the scent of incense burning nearby. Beside the gourd lay kola nuts, their deep brown shells glistening under the soft light, alongside a handful of alligator pepper pods. A garden egg, vibrant and symbolic, was placed next to the other items, completing the ensemble of traditional offerings.

Ikunnu's heart raced, but her expression remained calm, her eyes focused on the elders before her. Each item on the tray held deep cultural meaning, representing the blessings and unity this ceremony would seal.

The room fell silent as Ikunnu moved toward Chief Idowu, the soft rustle of her attire the only sound breaking the stillness. All eyes were on her, watching with bated breath, waiting to see whom she would choose. The air was thick with anticipation, each step she took amplifying the tension. As she approached Chief Idowu, her gaze was steady and sure, the murmur of voices faded completely.

She came to a halt before him, her face calm, betraying none of the nerves beneath. Slowly, with grace, she placed the ornately adorned tray on the floor between them. Her fingers wrapped around the calabash drinking gourd, and she lifted it, offering it to Chief Idowu. Her hands were steady, though her heartbeat rapidly in her chest.

Chief Idowu's wide smile broke the silence, his eyes twinkling with pride and satisfaction. The acceptance was clear before he even took the gourd, but when his large hand finally clasped it, a collective exhale rippled through the room.

The moment the calabash was in his hands, the room erupted to deafening applause. Voices cheered, and hands clapped, filling the space with joyful noise. Outside, the drummers responded instantly, their rhythm picking up, the vibrant beats echoing the celebration inside. The sound of the drums grew louder, faster, as if their energy mirrored the excitement of the moment.

Ikunnu remained poised, though a small smile crept onto her face as the weight of the ceremony lifted. She had made her choice. The elders nodded approvingly, and the guests swayed to the infectious beats as the celebration officially began.

Mr. Okeke, though still reserved, couldn't hide the small smile that crept across his face. The decision had been made, and the wedding would soon follow. As the celebration continued, there was a sense of inevitability in the air, a sense that this union, though sudden, was destined to bring both families together in prosperity and happiness.

Ikunnu could barely keep her excitement in check as she made her way back to campus. The memory of the knocking ceremony played over and over in her mind, the drumming, the cheering, and most of all, the way Chief Idowu had looked at her when she presented him with the calabash drinking gourd. It was a moment that marked the beginning of a new chapter in her life, one that promised opulence and status beyond her wildest dreams.

As she entered the residence, her friends were all in their usual spot, chatting and laughing. The moment she appeared, they sensed something was different. She couldn't hold it in any longer.

"Guess what, ladies!" Ikunnu announced, barely able to contain her joy.

Clara, Ifeyinwa, Adaobi, and Chinelo all looked up, sensing that something big was coming. "What is it?" Clara asked, her curiosity piqued.

Ikunnu took a deep breath, savoring the moment. "I'm getting married! And it's going to be a grand wedding. Chief Idowu has already begun the preparations, and I want all of you to be a part of it."

The room erupted in cheers and hugs as her friends congratulated her. "Wow, Ikunnu, that's amazing!" Adaobi exclaimed. "Tell us everything!"

Ikunnu's excitement was palpable as she continued, her voice brimming with enthusiasm. "I want you all to wear my ashebi," she said, her eyes glowing. "You're my inner clique, and I want everyone to know how special you are to me."

She pulled out fabric samples, holding up pieces of exquisite lace in vibrant purple and soft pink. "These are the colors," she explained, her fingers caressing the delicate material. "Lush, rich, and absolutely stunning. You can have them tailored into any style that suits you. I want each of you to stand out and feel beautiful. This is going to be a wedding to remember!"

The girls squealed with delight, already picturing themselves draped in luxurious fabrics, the center of attention at the wedding. Clara spun around, her arms outstretched as she imagined herself in ashebi. "This is going to be the wedding of the century!" she declared.

But as the initial excitement began to settle, a quiet thought crept into the back of Clara's mind. She exchanged a look with Ifeyinwa, who seemed to be thinking the same thing. The two of them had heard stories—whispers, really—about polygamous families and the challenges that came with them. Clara was the first to voice her concern.

"So, Ikunnu," she began, trying to keep her tone light, "have you met his other wives?"

The room grew a little quieter as the question hung in the air. Ikunnu hesitated, her smile fading just a touch. "Not yet," she admitted. "The first wife is in Lagos, and the second lives in Calabar. I haven't crossed paths with them, and to be honest, I'd prefer if it stayed that way."

Her friends exchanged glances, the weight of the situation beginning to settle in. Clara pressed on, her voice gentle but firm. "Ikunnu, it's important to know what you're getting into. How do you think they'll feel about you joining the family? And do they have children?"

Ikunnu sighed, her excitement dimming as reality started to intrude on her dreams. "I know, I know. It's just... Chief Idowu says everything will be fine. He's very respected, and he's assured me that his wives are aware and accepting of the situation. But I can't deny that I'm a little nervous."

Ifeyinwa nodded; her tone filled with concern. "It's not just about how they feel now; it's about how things will be in the future. You'll be part of a family, and that means navigating relationships that could be complicated, especially with children involved."

Chinelo, who had been quiet up until now, finally spoke. "Ikunnu, I'm happy for you, but you have to be careful. The first wife being in Lagos and the second in Calabar might seem like a blessing, but it could also mean you're isolated. What if they decide to visit? What if there are family gatherings?"

Clara, ever practical, leaned forward, her voice low. "You need to think about what happens after the wedding day. It's one thing to have a lavish ceremony, but what about the day-to-day? What if your paths cross? Are you ready for that?"

Ikunnu felt a pang of anxiety but pushed it aside. "I'll make sure to meet them before the wedding," she said, trying to reassure herself as much as her friends. "I'll find out more about them and their children. I hear the older kids from his first wife are all older than me. To be honest, I'm hoping to keep things as separate as possible. It might be best if our paths never cross."

The room was silent for a moment, the weight of her words hanging in the air. Then Clara smiled, reaching out to squeeze Ikunnu's hand. "We just want what's best for you. If you're happy, we're happy. But we'll be here for you no matter what happens."

Ikunnu smiled back, feeling a little more at ease. "Thank you, girls. I know this isn't going to be easy, but I'm determined to make it work. And with you all by my side, I know I can handle anything."

The girls nodded in agreement, their earlier concerns still lingering, but their loyalty to Ikunnu unwavering. They would be there for her through the excitement and the challenges, ready to support her every step of the way. For now, they chose to focus on the joy of the impending wedding, leaving the complexities of her future life as a wife to be dealt with when the time came.

Ikunnu even then, knew that marrying Chief Idowu meant entering into a complex family dynamic, and she was determined to navigate it with grace. To do that, she finally decided it was best to meet her two co-wives before the wedding. Understanding the nature of these women, who had already established their places in Chief Idowu's life, was crucial.

She was, however, clueless as to the best approach. Despite her usual boldness, the idea of meeting Chief Idowu's other wives before the wedding gave Ikunnu a real pause. Confrontation had never been an issue for her, she often thrived in situations where others might hesitate. But this wasn't a matter of being brash or fearless; it was about navigating an entirely new and delicate reality.

"I've never been in a situation like this," Ikunnu muttered, mostly to herself as she sat with her friends again. "How am I supposed to just walk in there and act like everything is fine? They're already established in the family, and I'm the new one coming in."

Adaobi leaned back in her chair; her arms crossed. "This isn't about fear, Ikunnu. It's about being smart. You don't want to go in there with guns blazing. You'll only make things harder for yourself."

"But what am I supposed to do? Play nice and hope they accept me?" Ikunnu shot back, her frustration bubbling up. "I don't want them thinking they can push me around just because I'm the last to join the party."

Clara gave her a gentle look. "No one's saying you should be passive. But remember, this is a family now, not just a competition. You need to find a way to assert yourself without causing unnecessary tension. Chief Idowu clearly wants harmony, so you have to show respect but still make it clear that you belong."

Ikunnu sighed, leaning forward and resting her chin on her hands. She was tough, sure, but this situation made her feel off balance.

"I'm used to just... going after what I want. Now I have to think about feelings, and family politics, and—ugh, I don't know!"

Ifeyinwa, ever the voice of reason, leaned in. "Maybe think of it like this: They're probably just as unsure about you as you are about them. You don't have to be their best friend, but you do have to set the tone for how you want the relationship to be."

Ikunnu shook her head slowly. "I hear you, but that's the part I don't get. What tone do I even set?"

Clara smiled, leaning closer. "One of quiet confidence. You don't have to make noise to prove you belong. Just be yourself—but a version of yourself that's aware of the dynamics. If you walk in there with the right mindset, they'll have no choice but to respect you."

Ikunnu sat back, her mind churning. For the first time in a long while, she felt like she was walking into something she couldn't control. But maybe that was the key, accepting that she couldn't control it and finding a way to make peace with that.

"Alright," she said finally. "I'll try. But don't expect me to start baking cookies for them or anything."

Her friends laughed, but the seriousness remained in the air.

Ikunnu gradually started to piece together the unspoken truth about the intricate dynamics in Chief Idowu's household. Although he lavished her with love, gifts, and the promise of a luxurious life, it became increasingly evident that none of it would matter if Olori Iyabo, the formidable first wife, did not approve. She had watched the way Chief Idowu deferred to Olori Iyabo in subtle but unmistakable ways, despite his efforts to project himself as the all-powerful head of the family.

Some stories were shared in hushed tones, from their friends or through maids who had witnessed it all over the years. There had been numerous women before her—beautiful, intelligent, and promising brides—who were swept into the fold by Chief Idowu's charm and wealth. Yet, some marriages were abruptly canceled days before the wedding, with no official reason given, though everyone knew why. Olori Iyabo, insulted or displeased by the smallest slight, had made it clear that these women would never truly be part of the family. She held the reins of influence tightly, and no decision was made without her quiet but firm approval.

Even more chilling were the stories of those women who had married Chief Idowu, only to find their unions unraveling within days. In one case, the bride's marriage collapsed in less than a week because she had unknowingly offended Olori Iyabo with a comment about her attire. Another was sent packing after a month, after failing to acknowledge Iyabo's superiority in the household. These tales left Ikunnu with a deep sense of unease.

She understood that her success as the newest wife was not dependent on the affection of Chief Idowu but on whether Olori Iyabo deemed her worthy.

Chief Idowu mentioned almost casually a few weeks later, that Olori Iyabo was due for hip replacement surgery but her only daughter, who had been planning to come home to care for her, was now unable to make it due to an emergency abroad.

"She'll be in the hospital for a few days," Chief Idowu had said, his brow furrowed in concern. "It's unfortunate, because she needs family around her."

At that moment, a light bulb went off in Ikunnu's mind. This was her chance, a route to bridge the gap between herself and the formidable first wife without it seeming forced or awkward. Without hesitation, she made the offer.

"I could stay with her at the hospital," Ikunnu had said, trying to sound nonchalant even though her heart was pounding. "I mean, I'm not doing much before the wedding. I could help her out."

Chief Idowu looked surprised, but then a smile spread across his face. "That's very kind of you, Ikunnu. I think she'd appreciate the company."

And so, a few days later, Ikunnu found herself walking into the private hospital where Olori Iyabo was recovering from her surgery. As she approached the room, nerves started to bubble in her stomach. For all her usual confidence, this felt different. The dynamic between wives—especially in a polygamous household—wasn't something you could charge into with her usual brashness. She would have to tread lightly.

When she entered the room, Olori Iyabo was sitting up in bed, her face a little drawn from the surgery, but her regal air intact. She glanced up at Ikunnu, her expression unreadable.

"Good afternoon, Ma," Ikunnu greeted, her voice soft but steady as she knelt in front of Olori Iyabo. She made sure to keep her tone respectful, trying her best to hide any trace of nervousness. "Chief mentioned you're in the hospital, and I thought I could keep you company for a while. If you're okay with that."

Olori Iyabo lay back in her hospital bed, her expression unreadable, her eyes sharp even in her weakened state. Ikunnu's heart raced, and for a moment, she regretted coming. The silence stretched on, and the sound of the hospital's machines felt deafening in the stillness. Had she overstepped? Perhaps Olori Iyabo didn't want visitors, least of all her husband's newest and youngest wife-to be.

Just as Ikunnu was about to apologize and leave, Olori Iyabo's eyes softened ever so slightly. She gave a small nod, barely perceptible but enough for Ikunnu to breathe a sigh of relief.

"Sit," Olori Iyabo said, her voice raspy yet commanding. "You may stay."

Ikunnu quickly settled into the chair beside the bed, thankful that her offer hadn't been rejected outright. She clasped her hands in her lap, glancing briefly at Olori Iyabo, who was now adjusting her blankets.

"I hope you're feeling better, Ma," Ikunnu ventured cautiously. "Chief has been very worried."

Olori Iyabo's lips curved slightly, though it wasn't quite a smile.

"Chief worries too much," she muttered, her tone dismissive but not unkind. "I've been through worse."

Ikunnu nodded, unsure of how to respond. She knew Olori Iyabo was a formidable woman, someone whose approval—or disapproval—carried immense weight in the family. This was her first time seeing her in such a vulnerable state, and yet, even now, Olori Iyabo exuded strength.

After a few moments, Olori Iyabo glanced at Ikunnu, her eyes scrutinizing her. "You came," she said slowly, as if the fact itself was surprising. "Most would not."

Ikunnu met her gaze and offered a small smile. "You're part of the family, Ma. I just want to help, however I can."

Olori Iyabo looked away for a moment, then back at her. "We'll see about that," she said quietly. Though her words carried no warmth, they also lacked the coldness Ikunnu had feared.

It wasn't much, but it was a start. Relieved, Ikunnu took a seat beside the bed, the tension eased a bit.

Olori Iyabo was in her sixties, and looked every inch, the undeniable matriarch, and despite her vulnerable situation, her posture and demeanor radiated a calm confidence that spoke of years of experience and influence.

Over the next few days, Ikunnu continued to visit Olori Iyabo, patiently waiting on her despite the fact that the older woman had paid helpers attending to her needs. At first, their conversations were polite and brief, revolving around small, inconsequential things—how the weather seemed especially humid or the steady comings and goings of the hospital staff. Ikunnu remained attentive, bringing fresh fruits and asking if Olori Iyabo needed anything, though it was clear that the elder wife was still keeping her at a distance.

As the days passed and Olori Iyabo continued regaining her strength, the guarded wall between them began to crack. Slowly, she started sharing more personal stories. One afternoon, as Ikunnu adjusted her pillows, Olori Iyabo began to talk about her children, fondly recalling their mischievous antics when they were younger. She shared bits of wisdom, learned over decades of marriage, and spoke of the complex dynamics of being Chief Idowu's first wife, balancing respect and authority while making room for others.

"It wasn't easy in the beginning," Olori Iyabo said one evening, her voice softer than Ikunnu had ever heard it. "Being the first wife comes with its own set of challenges. I had to set the standard, make sure things were in order. And then came the others—each one different, each with their own needs and expectations."

Ikunnu listened intently, sensing that beneath Olori Iyabo's tough exterior lay a woman who had faced and overcome countless obstacles. She saw now that this wasn't just about status, it was about survival, respect, and finding balance in an intricate web of relationships.

"I'm sure it was difficult," Ikunnu said gently, trying to find the right words. "You've kept everything together so well. I admire that."

Olori Iyabo's gaze never left Ikunnu's face as she responded. "It's not just about keeping things together, my dear. It's about understanding. Without that, there's only chaos. That's why I'm glad you came." She paused, her expression unreadable, but her voice held a rare softness. "It's important for us to understand each other, especially in a family like ours."

Ikunnu, who had spent many sleepless nights worrying about how she would fit into this already established hierarchy of wives, felt a quiet relief wash over her. Perhaps this was the opening she had hoped for—a chance to truly be accepted.

"Yes, I agree," Ikunnu replied, her voice careful, deliberate. She didn't want to overstep, but she knew the importance of these words. "I want to ensure that we all coexist peacefully, for the good of the family and ourselves."

Olori Iyabo's eyes flickered with something resembling approval, though her face remained composed. "Peace is important," she said, nodding. "But don't forget, Ikunnu, respect is the foundation. You give it to me, and you'll get it back. It is also important that everyone knows their place. You see, my dear, I've been with Chief for many years. I've seen wives come and go. But I've always been here, because I understand what it means to be the first wife."

Ikunnu felt a shiver run down her spine. The message was clear: Olori Iyabo was in charge, and any disruption to the status quo would not be tolerated. The older woman might have seemed calm and even frail, but Ikunnu could sense the iron will beneath the surface. It was obvious like she had already heard that Olori Iyabo had Chief Idowu's ear in most matters.

"I won't forget, Ma," Ikunnu assured her.

"Even then," Olori Iyabo continued with a faint smile. "You have to be patient, strong, and sometimes... quiet. But don't mistake quietness for weakness, Ikunnu. In this life, it's about knowing when to speak and when to let things be."

Ikunnu listened closely, absorbing every word. It was the first time she had truly connected with the older woman, and she realized there was much more to Olori Iyabo than the intimidating matriarch she'd heard about. There was wisdom in her words—a kind of guidance Ikunnu hadn't expected.

By the end of her stay, Ikunnu felt a shift in their relationship. There was still a long way to go, but she knew she had taken an important first step in earning Olori Iyabo's respect. As she left the hospital room, she couldn't help but smile. What had started as an awkward and daunting situation had turned into an unexpected opportunity to connect with the woman who had once seemed untouchable.

Ikunnu started relaxing a bit as she was slowly easing into getting integrated into the Idowu family. She also knew that incurring Olori Iyabo's wrath would make her life miserable, even if they don't share the same roof. The first wife was a force to be reckoned with, and Ikunnu made a mental note to tread carefully.

Next, she visited Ofonime, the second wife, who lived in Calabar. The atmosphere was markedly different from her interactions with Olori Iyabo.

Ofonime was in her early forties, a bubbly Efik woman with an infectious laugh and a warm, welcoming demeanor.

As soon as Ikunnu arrived, she was greeted by the rich aroma of spices and herbs. Ofonime led her into the dining room, where a spread of Calabar delicacies awaited. The centerpiece was a steaming pot of *Afang* soup, its rich, savory scent filling the room.

"I hope you're hungry," Ofonime said with a grin, dishing out a generous portion of the soup onto Ikunnu's plate. "You haven't lived until you've tried my *Afang*."

Ikunnu couldn't help but smile. The food was delicious, a testament to Ofonime's culinary prowess. The Afang soup was rich and flavorful, filled with tender meats and perfectly cooked vegetables. As they ate, Ofonime kept the conversation light, regaling Ikunnu with stories of her family and life in Calabar.

But beneath the cheerful surface, there was a subtle undercurrent to Ofonime's words. As they finished their meal, she leaned in a little closer, her tone becoming more serious.

"You know, in a family like ours, it's important that everyone knows their place," Ofonime said, echoing Olori Iyabo's earlier sentiment. "We all have our roles to play, and as long as we respect that, we'll get along just fine."

Ikunnu nodded, understanding the unspoken message. Ofonime might have been warm and welcoming, but she was no pushover. She had carved out her space in Chief Idowu's life, and she expected Ikunnu to respect that.

Ofonime's two children, both in their teens, were polite but kept their distance. They greeted Ikunnu with the respect owed to their future stepmother but quickly retreated to their rooms, leaving the women to talk.

"My kids are at that age," Ofonime said with a chuckle as she served Ikunnu another helping of Afang soup. "Teenagers—they're too cool for their own good. But they know their place in the family."

As the visit drew to a close, Ofonime reassured Ikunnu that she and her children would attend the wedding. "We'll be there, all of us," she said, her tone light, though Ikunnu sensed an underlying obligation.

Ikunnu felt a mix of gratitude and unease after the visits. The women had seemingly welcomed her with open arms, but their words were laced with subtle warnings. They had made it clear that while she was welcome, she needed to understand her place in the family hierarchy.

They had also promised to attend her wedding, but she couldn't shake the feeling that their attendance was more of a duty, likely mandated by Chief Idowu, than a genuine desire to celebrate her joining their family.

As Ikunnu prepared for her marriage, she knew that winning over these women—and by extension, their children—would be one of her biggest challenges. They had carved out their places in Chief Idowu's life long before she came into the picture, and now it was up to her to find her own without disrupting the delicate balance they had established.

The day of Ikunnu's wedding was nothing short of extraordinary. Her father's home, once a modest bungalow, had undergone a dramatic transformation in the months following the knocking ceremony. Now, it stood proudly as a grand one-storied building, its renovation was already the talk of the neighborhood. The sheer opulence of the new house left the neighbors in awe, but this was merely a prelude to the lavish affair that was to come.

The canopies set up for guests stretched over two entire streets, their interiors nothing less than spectacular. Lush draperies lined the walls, while air conditioners hummed softly, ensuring the guests were cool and comfortable despite the sweltering heat outside. The contrast between the vibrant energy of the festivities and the cool interiors was carefully crafted to provide an unforgettable experience.

Food and drink stands were placed strategically throughout the venue, each station offering an array of delicacies that represented the finest of Nigerian cuisine. The tantalizing aroma of freshly cooked jollof rice and pepper soup wafted through the air, mingling with the smoky scent of suya, the spicy roasted meat that was a crowd favorite. Tables were adorned with bowls of puff-puff, chin-chin, and other finger foods, giving the guests a variety of sweet and savory treats to enjoy as they mingled.

The drinks were just as varied and extravagant. Guests could choose from exotic cocktails mixed by skilled bartenders or traditional palm wine, served from ornate kegs into calabash bowls. Uniformed waitstaff moved elegantly through the crowd, offering a variety of beverages, ensuring no guest was left wanting.

The live music was another highlight of the day. A renowned Makossa dance band, known for their signature Afrobeat fusion, played, their rhythms pulling guests to the dance floor. Their infectious beats filled the air, blending seamlessly with the laughter and chatter of the crowd. The DJ, meanwhile, expertly alternated with the band, spinning the latest Afrobeats hits, keeping the energy high and the party buzzing.

Dancing groups, dressed in vibrant, traditional attire, also performed cultural dances that had guests clapping and cheering.

It was a true Owanbe, a grand celebration of Nigerian culture and community. Guests swayed effortlessly between the live rhythms of the band and the pulsating beats from the DJ, every song amplifying the festive mood. The dance floor was never empty, filled with the joyful movements of guests dressed in their finest attire. Women in beautifully embroidered ashebi and men in brightly colored agbadas twirled and laughed, adding their own rhythm to the vibrant pulse of the event.

As the day progressed, it was clear to everyone present that this was no ordinary wedding—it was a full-blown celebration of life, love, and wealth. Chief Idowu had spared no expense to ensure this day was one of the most talked about in recent memory.

"Can you believe this?" Clara whispered to Ifeyinwa as they navigated the bustling crowd, both dressed elegantly in the rich, lace ashebi, chosen by Ikunnu for her bridal party. The gold and teal fabric shimmered under the lights, perfectly complementing the grandeur of the event.

"I bet Ikunnu will be in her elements—this is her vibe totally."

Ifeyinwa chuckled, glancing around at the lavish decorations, the glittering chandeliers hanging from the canopies, and the impeccably dressed guests.

"Oh, absolutely. This is *so* Ikunnu. She was born for this kind of spotlight."

They exchanged knowing smiles, imagining their friend basking in the attention and luxury that surrounded them.

With live music filling the air, a DJ mixing the latest hits, and everyone dressed to impress, the scene was undeniably extravagant. For Ikunnu, it was the perfect backdrop for the beginning of her new life as Chief Idowu's wife, and Clara knew this was just the kind of grand occasion her friend had always dreamed of.

Ifeyinwa continued, her eyes wide with amazement. "Ikunnu really hit the jackpot with Chief Idowu. Look at all this! And to think, we were worried about her co-wives."

The two women exchanged knowing glances as they spotted Olori Iyabo and Ofonime, both dressed regally and surrounded by their children.

"I wonder what they're thinking," Adaobi said as she joined them, her eyes darting between the two older women. "They must know this is a big deal for Ikunnu. Even with all their experience, they can't help but be impressed."

"Maybe," Chinelo added, adjusting her gele, or hair scarf. "But I'm sure they also know their place in all this. Chief Idowu made sure of that."

As the women continued to chat, their attention was drawn to the arrival of more dignitaries, including some members of the senate, few governors, local chiefs, as well as some popular and well-known rich individuals, each one more impressive than the last. The air was thick with the scent of expensive perfumes and the soft rustle of luxurious fabrics as the guests made their way to their seats.

Ikunnu's parents, standing by the entrance, greeted everyone with wide smiles. They were dressed to the nines, and the pride in their eyes was unmistakable. They had every reason to be proud—their daughter was marrying into wealth and prestige, and the day had gone off without a hitch.

When Ikunnu finally made her entrance, the crowd fell silent, and then, almost as one, they gasped. Her dress was a masterpiece, a blend of traditional and modern styles that highlighted her beauty and grace. She moved with the poise of a queen, her every step a testament to the life she was about to begin.

"This is everything I ever dreamed of," Ikunnu whispered to herself as she caught sight of Chief Idowu waiting for her at the stand. The love in his eyes was evident, and she knew, despite the challenges ahead, that she had made the right choice.

As the ceremony proceeded, Clara leaned over to Adaobi. "This wedding… it's the talk of the town already. People will be talking about this for days, maybe weeks!"

Adaobi smiled, her eyes on Ikunnu and Chief Idowu. "It's everything she wanted and more. And you know what? She deserves every bit of it."

The day continued in a whirlwind of festivities, with dancing, laughter, and enough food to feed an army. As the sun set and the lights came on, casting a golden glow over the celebration, Ikunnu looked around at the life she was stepping into. It was grand, it was opulent, and it was hers. The wedding had been everything she had dreamt of and more, and as she took Chief Idowu's hand, she knew she was ready for whatever came next.

After their extravagant honeymoon in the Maldives, Chief Idowu soon set Ikunnu up in Abuja, where her life reached an entirely new level of luxury. The magnificent duplex in Maitama, with its soaring ceilings, gleaming marble floors, and a spacious garden filled with exotic flowers, became her palace. Every morning, she was greeted by the scent of freshly brewed coffee, courtesy of her personal chef, who prepared gourmet meals three times a day. Maids attended to her every need—ironing her clothes, organizing her ever-growing collection of luxury jewelry, and managing the household with effortless precision.

As Ikunnu settled into this life of opulence, her pregnancy began to advance, adding another layer of joy and anticipation to her already privileged world. The staff, ever vigilant, ensured she was well cared for during her pregnancy. Her meals were now more tailored to her needs, with the chef preparing nutrient-rich dishes to support her health and the baby's growth. Doctors regularly visited the house for check-ups, sparing her the need to go out in public unless she wished.

Her belly grew rounder with each passing week, and Ikunnu relished in the gentle attention she received. The excitement of becoming a mother, combined with the ease of her luxurious lifestyle, made her glow even more. Friends and family who visited couldn't help but comment on how radiant she looked. Every detail of her pregnancy was handled with meticulous care, and as her due date approached, plans were made for her to deliver in the United States, ensuring the best care for both her and the baby.

Travel remained a frequent part of her life, and despite the pregnancy, Ikunnu moved with the same ease and grace. Whether it was a shopping spree in Dubai or a quiet weekend in Paris, everything was arranged with care. Her bags were packed, her flights booked, and her itinerary organized without her having to lift a finger. Even during her travels, her pregnancy was never a burden.

Every hotel she stayed in ensured her comfort, providing special pillows, meals, and anything else she might need.

As her pregnancy advanced, so did the preparations for the baby. The nursery in her Maitama home was being designed by the best decorators, while custom-made furniture and clothes were shipped in from Europe. Chief Idowu spared no expense in ensuring that their child would be born into a life of luxury.

Ikunnu's life was perfect—a seamless blend of wealth, comfort, and the anticipation of motherhood. The journey she had taken from a university student dreaming of grandeur to a life of unimaginable luxury was something she couldn't help but reflect on. She had everything she ever wanted, and with a baby on the way, her life felt even more complete.

"Abuja suits you, Ikunnu," Ofonime remarked with a warm smile as she sipped on freshly made zobo in Ikunnu's airy living room. She was visiting with Ikunnu prior to her departure to the USA to deliver her baby. The atmosphere was light and joyful. The two women had grown closer over the months, often meeting for lunch or an easy chat, building a rapport that felt genuine despite the complexities of their shared family dynamics.

Ikunnu smiled, twirling the glass in her hand, savoring the tart sweetness of the zobo. "It has its perks, no doubt," she responded. "But you know how it is. I still have to be mindful of my place."

Ofonime nodded, her expression softening with understanding. She knew the intricacies all too well, having navigated the role of second wife for years. "Yes, especially with Olori Iyabo around. But you're doing well," she reassured. "Just keep a low profile at family functions, let her and I lead the way, and you'll be fine."

Ikunnu met her gaze and chuckled softly, a knowing smile playing on her lips. "That's a small price to pay," she said, her voice filled with quiet confidence. "As long as I can enjoy this life, I have no complaints."

The two women shared a moment of silent agreement.

Ofonime smiled, raising her glass. "Here's to a peaceful life and all its rewards."

Ikunnu clinked her glass against Ofonime's, her eyes gleaming with satisfaction. "Cheers to that."

Soon after the birth of her first child in the USA—a joyous occasion that brought both celebration and relief—Ikunnu began to carve out her own niche. She started trading in high-end jewelry and luxury bags, quietly building a business that was hers alone. It was her way of ensuring she had something to fall back on, just in case.

Her trips to New York became more frequent, especially as her business grew. During these visits, she never failed to drop in on Clara, Adaobi, Chinelo, and Ifeyinwa.

On one such visit, the four friends gathered in Clara's cozy apartment in Brooklyn. As they settled down with glasses of wine, the conversation inevitably turned to Ikunnu's new life in Abuja.

"So, you're really living the dream, huh?" Adaobi teased, her eyes wide with curiosity. "Chef, maids, a duplex in Maitama… What's it like?"

Ikunnu laughed, brushing off the question with a wave of her hand. "It's not all that glamorous, trust me. There's a lot to manage, and I have to be careful around my co-wives. But yes, it's comfortable."

"If by 'comfortable,' you mean living like a queen, then sure," Chinelo said, shaking her head in disbelief. "I can't even imagine it."

Clara, who had been quietly listening, leaned forward. "But how do you feel, Ikunnu? Really? Are you happy?"

Ikunnu paused, her smile softening. "I am. It's a different life, but it's a good one. And with the business I'm building, I feel like I'm doing something for myself, too."

Ifeyinwa nodded approvingly. "That's smart. You never know what could happen. It's good to have your own thing going."

The friends shared a moment of understanding, the reality of their different paths evident but not divisive. Despite the luxury that surrounded Ikunnu, she was still the same person at heart—ambitious, thoughtful, and determined to succeed on her own terms.

"Well, just know that we're here for you, no matter what," Clara said, squeezing Ikunnu's hand. "You'll always have us."

"And you can always count on us for some good old New York fun," Adaobi added with a grin.

Ikunnu smiled, feeling warmth in her chest that even the luxury of Abuja couldn't replicate. "I know. And that means the world to me."

CODA

Clara sat on the toilet seat, the pregnancy test clutched tightly in her hand, her heart pounding in her chest. It had been three long years since her fibroid surgery, three years filled with hope, despair, and endless prayers. This was her third IVF attempt, and the emotional toll of it all weighed heavily on her. The bathroom around her felt suffocating, the silence pressing in on her as she stared at the unopened package.

"You've been through worse, Clara. You can do this," she whispered to herself, trying to summon the strength she needed. Her thoughts drifted to Emeka, the man who had been her constant through it all. He was everything she had ever prayed for—loving, kind, steadfast. Through every disappointment, every tear-filled night, he had been there, holding her, reassuring her, never once wavering in his love for her.

"I just want to give him this one thing," she murmured, her voice thick with emotion. "Please, God, let this be it. Let this be the answer to all our prayers."

The fertility doctor had advised her to wait another week before testing, but Clara's patience had worn thin. The advertisements for the pregnancy tests boasted results as early as six days after conception, and she couldn't wait any longer. She hadn't even told

Emeka she was doing this today. What would he say if he knew? He'd probably tell her to wait, to follow the doctor's advice, but she just couldn't. The fear of another negative result gnawed at her, threatening to unravel the fragile hope she had carefully built.

As she slowly opened the test box, Clara's mind flashed back to the clinic, where the nurse had urged her to get up soon after the procedure. It was supposed to be a routine comment, but it had cut deep. Clara had resisted, stubbornly lying there with her hips thrust up, determined that gravity would somehow aid in her quest to conceive. The nurse had chuckled softly, trying to reassure her.

"People have sex and get up immediately, and they still have babies, you know."

Clara had nearly lost her composure. What did that nurse know?

Had she ever experienced the hollow ache of empty arms, the despair of a womb that refused to cooperate? Did she have an Emeka waiting at home, his eyes filled with hope every time she walked through the door? The questions had bubbled up, sharp and bitter, but Clara had forced them down, choosing instead to breathe deeply and let the anger pass.

Now, alone in the bathroom, Clara chuckled bitterly at the memory.

"She doesn't understand," she said aloud, shaking her head. "No one understands unless they've been here." She exhaled deeply, trying to release the tension coiled in her chest. She thought about all they had gone through—the surgeries, the treatments, the endless cycle of hope and heartbreak. And yet, here she was again, holding a tiny test in her hands, hoping against hope that this time would be different.

Finally, with a shaky hand, she took the test out of its packaging and held it up, staring at the small, innocuous-looking device as if it held all the power in the world. In a way, it did.

Her phone buzzed on the countertop, pulling her out of her thoughts. It was a message from Emeka. She picked it up, her heart skipping a beat as she read his words.

"Hey love, just checking in. How's your day going? Remember, no matter what, I'm here with you. Always."

Tears welled up in Clara's eyes, blurring her vision. He didn't know what she was about to do, but somehow, he always seemed to know when she needed reassurance. She didn't deserve him, she thought. But at the same time, she knew how much this meant to both of them. She had to know. She had to try.

With one last deep breath, she stood up, steadying herself. She could do this. She had to do this.

"Okay," she whispered, finally ready to face whatever the future held. "Here we go."

Minutes passed like hours as Clara sat there, unable to look at the test. Her heart raced, her breath shallow, as she willed herself to find the courage. Finally, with trembling hands, she glanced down at the little plastic device—and there they were. Two lines. It was positive.

Her heart leapt into her throat. For a moment, all she felt was pure, unfiltered joy. *It worked. It really worked!* But almost as quickly as the elation came, fear crept in. Was it too early? Could it be a false positive? She'd read stories about how sometimes the first test shows positive, only for hope to be dashed later. She couldn't bear the thought of raising Emeka's hopes for nothing. Not after everything they had been through.

Clara decided she wouldn't tell him yet. She would check again tomorrow, and then again on the day the doctor had recommended. She needed to be absolutely sure before she shared the news. Keeping this secret from Emeka would be hard, but she knew it was the right thing to do.

That evening, as they sat together in the living room, Emeka noticed something different about her. "You seem lighter tonight, Clara. Did something good happen?" he asked, his eyes full of warmth.

Clara smiled, a playful glint in her eye. "Maybe I'm just trying to stay positive," she teased, her heart fluttering with the double meaning behind her words. "After all, if I believe, then my chi will believe too."

Emeka chuckled, pulling her closer. "Well, whatever it is, I'm just glad to see you smile like this."

Clara rested her head on his shoulder, her heart filled with a mix of hope and nerves. She would have to wait a little longer to know for sure, but at that moment, wrapped in Emeka's embrace, she allowed herself to believe. Just a little.

As Clara wrapped a towel around herself, her mind was already racing with thoughts about the second pregnancy test. She had barely slept the night before, her mind churning with excitement and anxiety. She was desperate to know if yesterday's result was real, but as she reached for the test kit, her phone buzzed on the counter. It was Ifeyinwa.

She picked up the call, trying to mask the nervous energy in her voice. "Hey, Ifeyinwa, what's up?"

"Hello, Sis! Did you get the email invite?" Ifeyinwa's voice was bursting with excitement, the kind of excitement that made Clara's heart skip a beat.

"Which invite?" Clara asked, her mind still half on the test she was about to take.

"Adaobi's! She's getting married!" Ifeyinwa practically shouted.

Clara froze, her hand still hovering over the test kit. "Wait, what? Adaobi? Our Adaobi? Getting married?" she whooped, a huge grin spreading across her face. "Hold on, let me check this out!"

With her heart racing for an entirely different reason now, Clara fumbled for her phone, scrolling through her emails until she found it. There, in black and white, was a save-the-date invitation from Adaobi herself.

"Oh my God!" Clara exclaimed, her excitement bubbling over. "It's true! She's really getting married!"

The two friends launched into an animated conversation, their voices intertwining with laughter and disbelief. "I can't believe she kept this a secret! After all her shenanigans on those dates, she finally found her perfect match!" Clara said, shaking her head in amazement. "And it's Chidi? How on earth did they reconnect? She didn't say a word about it!"

"I know, right?" Ifeyinwa responded, her tone equally amazed. "This is such a surprise. I always thought she'd give us a play-by-play of her love life, but this? This is out of nowhere!"

Clara couldn't stop smiling. She could picture Adaobi, always so full of life, finally finding the love she deserved. After all the years of dating mishaps, awkward introductions, and outright disasters, it seemed almost surreal that Adaobi had found someone who could keep up with her.

But as their excitement simmered down, Clara's thoughts turned to Ifeyinwa. "How are you holding up, Ifeyinwa? It's been a lot lately."

There was a pause at the other end of the line, and when Ifeyinwa spoke again, her voice was quieter, weighed down by the burden she was carrying. "Clara, it's been tough. I finally started taking my Licensure exams now that Mom's here to help with the kids, but… there's something else."

Clara felt her heart tighten. "What is it?"

"Christopher… he fathered a child with Latoya. His paper wife," Ifeyinwa said, the words heavy with betrayal. "And instead of divorcing her like he said he would, he's decided to stay with her. I feel so… betrayed."

"Oh, Ifeyinwa…" Clara whispered, her heart breaking for her friend. "I'm so sorry."

"Thank you," Ifeyinwa replied, her voice steady despite the pain. "But I can't dwell on it. I need to focus on my exams, on getting through this. I need to be able to take care of myself and the kids. Husband or no husband."

Clara felt a wave of admiration wash over her. Ifeyinwa's strength was palpable, her determination unwavering. "You're so strong, Ifeyinwa. And you're going to get through this. You're going to be an amazing doctor, and no matter what happens with Christopher, you'll have your own back."

"Thanks, Clara. That means a lot," Ifeyinwa said, a hint of gratitude softening her voice.

As Clara and Ifeyinwa were about to wrap up their conversation, Ifeyinwa's voice softened with concern. "Clara, before we go, how's everything going with your fertility treatment? I've been thinking about you."

Clara paused, her heart suddenly heavy with the secret she was holding. She hadn't planned on sharing this with anyone, not until she was absolutely sure. But this was Ifeyinwa—her friend, her sister, and a doctor who understood the complexities of what she was going through.

Taking a deep breath, Clara decided to let Ifeyinwa in.

"Well… I did a test yesterday," she started, her voice a mix of excitement and fear. "And it was positive."

There was a brief silence on the other end of the line, and then Ifeyinwa's voice came through, filled with cautious optimism.

"Clara, that's amazing news! How do you feel?"

"I don't know," Clara admitted, her voice trembling. "I'm excited, but I'm also scared. What if it's too early? What if it's a false positive? I was just about to take another test when you called."

"Do it now," Ifeyinwa urged gently. "I'll stay on the line. Whatever happens, I'm here with you."

Clara nodded, even though Ifeyinwa couldn't see her. With shaky hands, she picked up the second test and went through the motions again, her heart pounding the entire time. When the result finally appeared, it was the same—two lines, another positive.

"I… it's positive again," Clara whispered, a mix of relief and disbelief washing over her.

Ifeyinwa let out a breath she hadn't realized she was holding.

"Clara, this is a good sign. But I understand why you're cautious. It's okay to wait for the next test, just to be sure. But for now, just breathe. This is a moment to hold onto."

Clara nodded, feeling a wave of gratitude for Ifeyinwa's steady support. "Thank you, Ifeyinwa. I'm still going to wait for the test next week before I tell Emeka. I just need to be sure."

"I get it," Ifeyinwa said warmly. "And when you're ready, you'll have the best news to share with him. Until then, take care of yourself, okay?"

As they finally ended the call, Clara felt a little more at ease. She wasn't alone in this—she had her sisters, and that made all the difference. However, despite her obvious excitement, the mix of emotions was intense. The joy of Adaobi's impending wedding clashed with the sorrow and betrayal Ifeyinwa was facing, and it all felt a bit overwhelming. Yet beneath the swirl of emotions, Clara felt a deep sense of sisterhood, of the unbreakable bond she shared with these women. They were her anchor, her constant in a world full of uncertainties.

Clara picked up the phone again, her mind buzzing with questions. As soon as Ifeyinwa had mentioned Adaobi's upcoming wedding, Clara's curiosity had gone into overdrive. How could Chidi, the same Chidi who had ghosted Adaobi years ago, suddenly reappear and sweep her off her feet again? Something didn't add up.

"Congratulations, Adaobi!" Clara started, her voice cheerful but with a hint of urgency. "I'm so happy for you, but you have to tell me—how on earth did this happen? How did Chidi manage to worm his way back into your life?"

Adaobi sighed, the weight of the story clear in her tone. "Thank you, Clara. I'm still trying to wrap my head around it myself." She hesitated for a moment. "It's a long story, but I'll give you the short version."

"Please do, because I need to understand how this man, who vanished without a trace, is now your fiancé," Clara pressed, her skepticism barely concealed.

"Well," Adaobi began, "we lost touch after he disappeared on me. I was devastated, but I moved on—or at least I thought I had. Then, out of nowhere, I got this Facebook message: Hello Adaobi, this is Chidi. Remember me?'"

Clara snorted. "Remember him? As if you could forget the guy who shattered your heart and left you hanging. So, what did you do? Please tell me you didn't just fall for it."

"Clara, I didn't know what to think," Adaobi admitted, her voice tinged with frustration. "His profile had no pictures, no posts—it looked like he'd just made the account. I was suspicious, of course. I ignored the message for a few days, thinking if it was really him, he'd have to do better than that. I wasn't going to make it easy for him, not after what he did."

"You're right not to," Clara agreed, her tone sharpening. "He should've known better than to think he could just waltz back into your life with a lame message like that."

"Well, he did try again," Adaobi continued, her voice softening. "He sent another message, apologizing for everything. He explained why he disappeared and asked if we could talk. I didn't respond right away, but I was curious. Eventually, I gave in, and we ended up having a long conversation."

Clara couldn't hide her disbelief. "And that was enough for you? A conversation after all these years?"

Adaobi's temper flared. "It wasn't just one conversation, Clara. We talked for months. He was persistent, and he explained a lot. It wasn't simple, and it definitely wasn't easy for me to forgive him. But I did, because I wanted to. And now we're getting married."

Clara's voice turned icy. "I just hope you know what you're doing, Adaobi. Men like Chidi don't just change overnight. You're taking a big risk."

"I appreciate your concern, Clara, but I know what I'm doing," Adaobi shot back, her irritation clear. "Chidi has changed, and I'm happy. Isn't that what matters?"

Clara took a deep breath, trying to rein in her emotions. "Of course, Adaobi. Your happiness is what's most important. I just don't want to see you hurt again."

Adaobi's voice softened. "I know, Clara. And I appreciate that. But this time, it's different. I believe in second chances, and I'm willing to give Chidi his."

Clara forced a smile, though Adaobi couldn't see it. "Okay, then. I'll support you, whatever happens. But you know the girls are going to want every detail when we see you."

Adaobi laughed, the tension easing. "I'll be ready for them. And I'll make sure to have some wine on hand, because it's going to be a long night of storytelling."

Clara chuckled, though a part of her still felt uneasy. "I'm looking forward to it. Just promise me one thing, Adaobi—promise me you'll keep your eyes open."

"I promise, Clara," Adaobi said, her tone reassuring. "I'm not going into this blindly. But I also won't let fear hold me back from happiness."

Clara nodded, finally letting go of her worries for the moment.

"That's all I needed to hear. I'm with you, Adaobi, no matter what."

"Thanks, Clara. That means the world to me," Adaobi replied, her voice warm again.

As they hung up, Clara couldn't shake the feeling that there was more to the story than Adaobi was letting on. But for now, all she could do was hope that her friend's faith in Chidi wasn't misplaced.

Soon after the phone conversation with Adaobi, Clara felt a mix of nerves and exhilaration following the events of the day. She reclined on the couch, her hand instinctively moving to her stomach.

"Babies…," she murmured, the word almost magical. What if all three embryos had taken? The idea of triplets made her heart race. Even twins, or just one baby, would be more than she had dared to hope for.

As she lay there, lost in thought, she absentmindedly rubbed her tummy. For a moment, she could have sworn she felt a tiny flutter—a kick, maybe? She laughed out loud, a sound filled with pure delight. "Clara, you're being ridiculous," she chided herself gently, knowing it was too soon for such things. But the joy bubbling inside her was too intense to ignore. She refused to let anything—doubt, fear, or caution—cloud her happiness right now.

She moved to the kitchen, her feet almost gliding over the floor as she hummed a tune, she couldn't quite place. The kitchen, usually just a part of her routine, felt like a space of new beginnings tonight. She chopped vegetables with a rhythm that matched her heartbeat, her thoughts drifting to Emeka.

His smile, his kindness, his unwavering support, they had been through so much together. And yet, here she was, holding the biggest secret of their lives, not quite ready to share it.

"Not yet," she whispered, stirring the pot on the stove. She could picture his face when she finally told him, the way his eyes would light up with hope, with love. But she wasn't ready to let him into her bubble of joy just yet. She didn't want to see that light fade if something went wrong. No, she needed to be sure—absolutely sure.

She set the table, every detail perfect, just as Emeka liked it. As she placed the last dish, Clara stood back, admiring her work. She knew he'd notice something was different, but she was prepared to deflect his questions, at least for a little while longer. This moment, this secret, was hers for now.

With a deep breath, she sat down to wait for him, her hand resting once again on her belly. The excitement was still there, humming beneath the surface. She smiled to herself, letting the joy wash over her. This was her time, and she wasn't going to let anything spoil it.

On the other hand, and as Clara had predicted about the other ladies demanding explanations from Adaobi, Chinelo called Adaobi the next day. Her voice rang with excitement as soon as Adaobi picked up the call.

"Adaobi! Oh, my goodness, I just heard the news! You're getting married! Congratulations, Nnem!"

Adaobi couldn't help but smile at her friend's enthusiasm. "Thanks, Chinelo! It's still sinking in, honestly. I'm really excited."

"I'm sure you are! But I have to admit, when Clara told me, I was like, 'Wait, what? Chidi? How did that even happen?' You've got to give me the full gist!"

Adaobi's smile faltered slightly. "I've been getting a lot of that," she said with a hint of irritation. "I thought you guys would be happy for me, not throwing a million questions my way."

"We are happy for you, Adaobi," Chinelo said quickly, her voice softening. "But you have to understand, after everything you went through with Chidi back in university, we're just worried, that's all. We care about you."

"I know you do," Adaobi replied, her tone still a bit defensive. "But you guys also know I wouldn't be doing this if it wasn't for the right reasons."

"Of course, we trust you," Chinelo said. "So, tell me what happened. How did Chidi come back into your life after all this time?"

Adaobi sighed, collecting her thoughts before launching into the story. "It's a long story, but here goes. Back in university, Chidi had to leave because of me. He was involved with a cult, and they found out how much I meant to him. He knew they could use me to get to him, so he did the only thing he could to protect me—he left. His parents got him out of the country immediately, and he moved to the USA. Since he was born there, it wasn't too hard for him to settle in Houston. He went on to finish an IT program and now works as an IT analyst at Microsoft."

Chinelo listened intently, not interrupting as Adaobi continued.

"But even after all these years, he couldn't forget about me," Adaobi said, her voice softening as she spoke. "He tried to move on, but he couldn't. He never found anyone else he could commit to because he was still in love with me. For years, he wanted to reach out but didn't know how to find me. Eventually, a friend suggested he try Facebook, and that's when he finally sent me a message. At first, I didn't even know if it was really him."

"Wow, Adaobi," Chinelo said, her voice filled with surprise. "That must have been such a shock."

"It was," Adaobi admitted. "I didn't respond at first because I wasn't sure if it was even real. But when he sent another message, I decided to hear him out. We started talking, and it was like no time had passed between us. We've been visiting each other for almost a year now, and things just fell back into place. This isn't something I'm rushing into, Chinelo."

"I can see that now," Chinelo said thoughtfully. "And I'm really sorry if we came across as skeptical. It's just that we've always wanted the best for you, especially after how hurt you were when he disappeared."

"I know you mean well," Adaobi said, her voice softening a bit more. "But it's frustrating when I feel like I have to justify my happiness to my closest friends. I'm not the same person I was back then, and neither is Chidi. We've both grown a lot, and we're making this decision together with our eyes wide open."

Chinelo paused for a moment, taking in everything Adaobi had said.

"You're right, Adaobi. We shouldn't have doubted you. If you're happy, then we're happy for you. We just wanted to make sure you were okay, given everything you've been through."

"I appreciate that, Chinelo," Adaobi said, feeling a bit lighter. "And I really do want you guys to be part of this with me. I need your support, not just your questions."

"You've got it, girl," Chinelo promised. "We're here for you, no matter what. And you better believe we're going to make sure this wedding is everything you've ever dreamed of."

Adaobi finally let out a genuine laugh. "I'm counting on that. And thank you, Chinelo. It means a lot to know you're in my corner."

"Always, Adaobi," Chinelo said warmly. "Now, let's get to work on making this wedding the event of the century. You deserve nothing less."

Adaobi, feeling the warmth of their conversation, shifted the focus to Chinelo. "But enough about me, Chinelo. We've been talking so much about my wedding and Chidi—how are you? How's everything on your end?"

Chinelo paused, her tone softening. "You know, Nnem, things have actually been improving for us too. Osi finally agreed to seek help, and we've started couples' therapy. It's really making a difference in our relationship."

Adaobi's eyes lit up with genuine happiness for her friend. "That's amazing, Chinelo! I know how much you've been hoping for this. How's he doing with it?"

Chinelo let out a small sigh, reflecting on their journey. "It's been a process, but I'm proud of him for taking this step." Her tone soon shifted to a more reflective space, her earlier intensity fading into something softer, more introspective. "You know, the therapist thinks Osi's been struggling with depression for a long time," she continued quietly. "And when she started digging into his past, it really made me see things differently. She talked about how witnessing his father beat his mother when he was just a kid... how that might have left a bigger mark on him than we realized."

"Oh wow." Adaobi muttered in disbelief.

"You know how they say, *"hurt people, hurt people," and so does the abused become the abuser later in life.*" Chinelo paused, letting the weight of those words sink in. "It's starting to make sense. His behavior... it wasn't just him being difficult or weird, it was like he was carrying something heavy that neither of us fully understood. All that anger, the outbursts, the mood swings—it was deeper than I ever thought."

Adaobi frowned, processing the new perspective. "I always thought Osi had a bit of an edge, but depression? That explains so much more."

"Exactly!" Chinelo said, her voice soft but filled with a certain clarity.

"I didn't get it at first. I just thought maybe he was going through something temporary. But looking back now, his behavior was all over the place, like he was battling something inside. It was like he'd put up walls, and no matter what I did, I couldn't get through to him. He'd shut down completely some days or explode over the smallest things. I thought it was me, you know? But now... now I see it wasn't."

"If he grew up seeing his dad like that, it makes sense that it affected him more than you both realized," Adaobi added softly, her voice laced with empathy. "That kind of trauma doesn't just go away. It shapes you, sometimes in ways you don't even notice until much later."

Chinelo sighed, nodding in agreement. "Yeah, and I think Osi's been in denial about it for a long time. But now, at least, with the therapy, it's like the pieces are falling into place. I'm finally starting to understand why he acted the way he did. And honestly, it's helping me too. Seeing that it wasn't just him being *difficult*, but that he's been fighting something from his past. It's giving me more compassion, even though it's been hard."

Adaobi wished that she could reach out and hug her friend. "It sounds like you're both working through it, though. That's what matters."

Chinelo smiled faintly. "Yeah. I mean, it's not easy, but understanding where it comes from certainly helps. Now I know it's not just about *us* or the relationship, it's about him, and what he's been carrying all these years. We've still got a long way to go, but at least now we're facing it head-on." After a fleeting pause, Chinelo continued, "The therapist also suggested Osi sees a psychiatrist for medication, but he is not comfortable with that—he's completely against taking any psychotropic drugs."

Adaobi nodded, understanding the complexity of the situation. "I can imagine that's a tough decision for him. But just the fact that he's in therapy and working on things with you is such a positive step."

"Yes, and it's going much better than I had expected," Chinelo admitted. "Osi is more present, more engaged. We're finally talking again, really talking, and I think we're starting to reconnect in a way we haven't in years."

"I'm so happy to hear that," Adaobi said sincerely. "I know how much this means to you. It sounds like you're both really putting in the work."

"We are," Chinelo replied, her voice gaining a bit of strength. "And there's more good news. We recently got a financial windfall. Remember that guy who only paid half of what he owed us for the house? Out of the blue, he contacted us to pay the rest of the money. With that, we were finally able to put a down payment on our own house."

Adaobi's eyes widened with excitement. "Chinelo, that's incredible! After everything you've been through, you both deserve some good fortune. I'm so happy for you."

"It really felt like a blessing," Chinelo said, her voice brimming with relief. "And I've decided to start taking some access courses so I can enroll in nursing school. It's something I've wanted to do for a long time, and now I'm finally making it happen."

Adaobi's heart swelled with pride for her friend. "You're going to be an amazing nurse, Chinelo. You've always had such a big heart and a natural way of caring for others. This suits you perfectly."

"Thank you, Adaobi," Chinelo said, her voice tinged with emotion. "It's been a long road, but I finally feel like I'm moving in the right direction."

Adaobi smiled, her voice warm. "And what about Osi? How's he handling everything with you going back to school?"

Chinelo chuckled softly. "He's been supportive, thankfully. He's actually contemplating starting a trading business and travelling between Nigeria and the USA. He's still in the planning stages, but it's something he's passionate about."

"That's great to hear," Adaobi said, genuinely thrilled for her friend. "It sounds like you both have a lot of exciting things ahead. I'm really happy that things are turning around for you."

Chinelo's voice softened as she replied, "Thank you, Adaobi. It's been a tough journey, but we're finally seeing some light. And I have to say, hearing about your happiness with Chidi just adds to the joy. We've all been through so much, and it's nice to finally have some good news to share."

Adaobi felt a deep sense of connection with Chinelo in that moment. "We've been through a lot, haven't we? But it's moments like this that make it all worth it. I'm so grateful for your friendship, Chinelo. And I'm even more excited that we're both heading into better times."

"Absolutely Nnem," Chinelo agreed, her voice filled with warmth. "And you know we're going to make your wedding the celebration of the century, right? You deserve nothing but the best."

Adaobi laughed, her heart lightened by the support and love she felt from her friend. "I'm counting on it! And thank you, Chi, for everything. It means the world to me to have you in my corner."

"Always, Adaobi," Chinelo replied, her voice full of affection. "We're all in this together, and we're going to make sure you have the happiest wedding day ever. Just wait and see."

As they ended the call, Adaobi felt a profound sense of gratitude. Not only was she excited about her own future, but she was also deeply moved by the positive changes in her friends' lives. The bonds they shared were stronger than ever, and as they each moved forward on their paths, Adaobi knew that they would continue to support and uplift one another, no matter what.

Over at her usual corner at the St. Elizabeth Library, Ifeyinwa was surrounded by textbooks and flashcards. The silence of the library was comforting, a sharp contrast to the chaos in her mind as she prepared for the USMLE Step 1 exams. The pressure was immense, but she had no choice. This was her ticket to reclaiming her future, her independence.

She had just sent a congratulatory message to Adaobi instead of calling her directly. Chinelo's words echoed in her mind: *"Don't bombard her with questions, Ify. She's probably overwhelmed as it is. Let her come to you when she's ready."*

So, Ifeyinwa had done just that, keeping her message light and promising to call later. As she returned to her studies, flipping through pages of notes, she suddenly remembered that Clara was supposed to repeat another pregnancy test today.

A wave of concern washed over her. Clara had been through so much, and Ifeyinwa knew how much this meant to her. She glanced at her phone. No messages from Clara yet. *What's going on?"* she thought, anxiety creeping in. Without hesitating, she dialed Clara's number.

Clara picked up on the second ring, her voice bubbling with excitement that Ifeyinwa hadn't heard in a long time.

"Ify! Oh my God, Ify!" Clara's voice was almost breathless.

"Clara, what's going on? Did you take the test?" Ifeyinwa asked, her own heart was pounding now.

"I did!" Clara exclaimed. "And it's positive, Ify! Strongly positive! I can't believe it!" Her words tumbled out in a rush, as if she had been holding them in for too long.

Ifeyinwa felt a flood of relief and joy for her friend. "Clara, that's amazing! I'm so happy for you. I knew it, I just knew it!"

Clara was practically glowing through the phone. "I already texted Emeka! He's on his way home now. I couldn't wait to tell him. Ify, I'm so excited, I don't even know what to do with myself!"

Ifeyinwa smiled, leaning back in her chair. "You deserve this happiness, Clara. After everything you've been through, this is your moment."

"Thank you, Ify," Clara said, her voice softening with emotion. "I still can't believe it. I keep staring at the test, just to make sure it's real."

"It's real, Clara. And it's going to be amazing." Ifeyinwa's voice was filled with reassurance. Despite her own troubles, this moment was all about Clara, and she was genuinely happy for her friend.

As they talked, Clara shared how she had already started planning how to tell Emeka in person, even though she'd texted him the news.

"I just couldn't help myself. He's going to be over the moon, Ify. I can't wait to see his face."

"I can imagine," Ifeyinwa laughed softly. "But don't stress yourself out, okay? Take it easy, rest up, and just enjoy this moment. You've earned it."

Clara sighed happily. "I will, I promise. And Ify... thank you. For always being there."

"Always," Ifeyinwa replied, her voice gentle. "Now go and enjoy your good news. We'll talk more later, okay?"

As she hung up the phone, Ifeyinwa felt warmth spread through her. Clara's joy was infectious, and for a moment, it made the weight on her own shoulders feel a little lighter. She looked around the quiet library, thinking about the long road ahead, but also about the small victories that made everything worthwhile. With a smile, she picked up her pen and got back to work, fueled by the happiness of her friend's long-awaited miracle.

When Emeka walked through the front door, he immediately sensed something different in the air. Clara stood in the hallway, trying to suppress a smile, but the glint in her eyes gave her away. Before she could say anything, Emeka crossed the room in a few quick strides, lifting her off her feet and spinning her around.

"Tell me it's true," he murmured against her neck before setting her down gently.

Clara couldn't hold back any longer. "It's true, Emeka. We're pregnant!"

Emeka's face lit up with a joy that seemed to fill the entire room. He kissed her, his excitement overflowing. "Clara, we did it! We really did it!" He wrapped her in a tight embrace, his voice choked with emotion. "I knew it, I just knew it would happen."

They stood there for a moment, holding each other, both overwhelmed with happiness. Emeka finally pulled back slightly, his hands still on Clara's shoulders, his eyes searching hers. "Have you called the clinic? When's our next appointment?"

"I called already. We have a follow-up appointment in a few days," Clara replied, still smiling. "They'll do more tests to confirm, but Emeka, it's really happening. We're going to be parents."

Emeka let out a breath he didn't realize he'd been holding. "We have everything we ever wanted," he said softly, almost as if he was afraid saying it out loud would break the spell.

Clara nodded, her eyes welling up. "We really do."

Later that evening, as they sat together on the couch, Clara filled Emeka in on the updates from her friends.

"You won't believe what's been going on with everyone," she began, resting her head on his shoulder.

"Tell me," Emeka said, still in a blissful daze, his arm around her.

"Well, Ifeyinwa's been studying like crazy for her USMLE exams," Clara started. "But she's dealing with a lot. Christopher—her husband—he's fathering a new baby with Latoya, the woman he married for papers. It's a mess, Emeka. I feel so bad for her, but she's handling it like a champ. She's determined to pass her exams and secure her own future, with or without him."

Emeka frowned. "That's tough. I always thought Christopher was more reliable. But I'm glad Ifeyinwa is focusing on herself. She's a strong woman. She'll get through this."

"She will," Clara agreed. "And then there's Chinelo. Her husband finally agreed to couples' therapy. They've been struggling, but it seems like he's really committed to working things out. Chinelo is also preparing to study nursing. She wants to do something for herself, something that gives her independence."

"That's good to hear," Emeka said thoughtfully. "Therapy could be the turning point they need. And I think nursing will be great for Chinelo. She's always been so caring. It suits her."

Clara smiled, thinking of her friend's determination. "Yeah, I think so too. And then there's Adaobi. She's getting married!"

Emeka raised his eyebrows. "Adaobi? Finally! Who's the lucky guy?"

"Remember Chidi? The one who disappeared from her years ago?" Clara said, watching Emeka's reaction.

Emeka's eyes widened. "The same Chidi? He came back?"

"He did," Clara confirmed, grinning. "It's a crazy story. He found her on Facebook out of nowhere, and they reconnected. Now they're getting married. I'm so happy for her. She's been through so much, and it's about time she found someone who appreciates her."

"That's incredible," Emeka said, shaking his head in disbelief. "Life is full of surprises."

"And speaking of surprises," Clara continued, "I heard from Ikunnu. She's visiting the U.S. in a few weeks."

"Another baby on the way?" Emeka teased.

Clara laughed. "No, no more babies for her. She already has two little girls and a boy now. She says she's done and is just going to enjoy her life. She's living the rich life in Abuja and seems really happy."

Emeka chuckled. "Good for her. It sounds like she's got everything under control. I'm glad all of you are thriving in your own ways."

Clara leaned back, feeling content and grateful. "You know, Emeka, we're all so different, but we've managed to stay close and support each other through everything. I think that's pretty special."

Emeka nodded, pulling her closer. "You're right. All five of you have been through so much, and yet you're all finding your own paths, your own happiness. We're lucky, Clara. So, so lucky."

Clara sighed, feeling a deep sense of peace. "We really are," she said softly, resting her head on Emeka's chest, listening to the steady beat of his heart. In that moment, with the love of her life by her side and the future looking brighter than ever, Clara knew that no matter what challenges lay ahead, they would face them together. And that was more than enough.

P. S.

Clara was the first of their friend's clique to arrive, her twin-filled belly preceding her like a badge of pride and impending motherhood. The doctor had firmly advised bedrest, insisting she stay off her feet as much as possible, but there was no way Clara could miss Adaobi's wedding. Nothing could have kept her away from this moment. She had been waiting for years to see her friend find her happily-ever-after, and she wasn't about to let a doctor's orders—or her growing discomfort—stand in the way. Still, caution whispered in her mind, and she'd made up her mind to leave right after the church service, not wanting to push her luck or risk the health of her precious "buns in the oven."

Adaobi's wedding plans had taken everyone by surprise. First, it had been postponed with no explanation. Then, for months, they'd heard nothing—no updates, no communication. The silence had weighed heavily on their minds, stirring concern and curiosity. But then, out of the blue, Adaobi had reached out last week with a new plan: she was having a much smaller, intimate wedding in a quaint chapel in Manhattan, inviting only her closest friends and family. The grand celebration they'd all imagined had been scaled back, and Clara had questions—so many questions. What had happened? Why the sudden shift? Why had Adaobi gone silent for so long?

The questions buzzed in Clara's mind, begging to be asked. But she held back, remembering all too well how defensive Adaobi had become the last time they'd tried to dig too deeply into her relationship with Chidi.

Adaobi had grown upset, her walls going up the moment they pressed her for details. Clara didn't want to repeat that. Today wasn't about satisfying her curiosity or getting an answer, it was about being there for her friend on one of the most important days of her life. So, despite the questions swirling in her mind, Clara resolved to smile, support Adaobi, and celebrate her in the way she deserved, leaving everything else for another day.

As Clara made her way to the front pews, she immediately noticed the subtle elegance of the church. Soft sunlight filtered through stained glass windows, casting colorful patterns on the floor. The pews were meticulously arranged, with name tags placed on each seat. Her heart skipped a beat when she spotted the familiar names—Clara, Ifeyinwa, Chinelo, and Ikunnu—on the second row, all on the bride's side. A warm sense of belonging filled her. The two sides of the church had been clearly divided, one for the groom's guests and the other for the bride's guests.

Just as Clara began to settle in, she couldn't help but notice a significant number of white guests on the groom's side. A quick glance around the room confirmed it—almost half of the people sitting there were white. *Was Chidi biracial?* The thought crossed her mind, and she found herself puzzled. She didn't know Chidi personally, but surely, if he were of mixed race, Adaobi would have mentioned it in one of their countless conversations over the years.

That was too important a detail to have slipped through. A subtle curiosity bubbled within her, but she pushed it aside for now.

The delicate hum of conversation and the rustling of elegant fabrics filled the room as more guests arrived. Suddenly, the distinct koi-koi sound of heavy heels tapping purposefully against the polished church floor caught Clara's attention. Even before turning around, she knew it had to be her cousin, Ikunnu.

Only Ikunnu could make such a grand entrance with just the sound of her heels. Clara turned her head, and there she was—stunning, as always.

Ikunnu moved with an air of confidence, her chocolate-brown gown hugging her figure in all the right places. The gown, though simple in design, shimmered under the light, catching the attention of those around her. Clara admired the way Ikunnu managed to make the color code—any shade of brown—look so effortlessly chic. As Ikunnu approached, her signature Channel No. 5 perfume wafted through the air, a scent Clara could recognize anywhere.

"Clara, my dear!" Ikunnu beamed, leaning in for a quick embrace before taking her seat beside her. The two exchanged a few words, both excited yet curious about the day ahead. Clara couldn't help but smile as Ikunnu settled into her spot, her presence always adding a touch of glamor to any occasion.

The anticipation in the room continued to build. Soon, all eyes would be on Adaobi and Chidi, and Clara found herself eager to see how the rest of the day would unfold.

Ifeyinwa and Chinelo glided into the pews, their beige gowns flowing gracefully as they exchanged smiles with Clara and Ikunnu. The soft fabric of their dresses shimmered under the chapel lights, catching the delicate gold accents on their jewelry. The four friends were now seated together, a silent but strong presence among the growing crowd of guests. The chapel, with its intimate setting and high-arched windows, was filling quickly. Murmurs of excitement filled the air, yet the friends remained quiet, exchanging only glances.

Clara's gaze wandered once more to the groom's side, and the sight made her brow furrow. The sheer number of white guests still surprised her, and she wasn't the only one. Ifeyinwa leaned in, whispering, "Are we sure we're at the right wedding?" Her voice was half-joking, but the hint of curiosity in her eyes betrayed her disbelief.

"I don't know... Adaobi would've mentioned something, right?" Chinelo added softly, her eyes fixed on the unfamiliar faces across the aisle.

Before they could continue their whispered musings, the room fell quiet. The faint strumming of a harp filled the air, the delicate notes drifting up to the vaulted ceilings. It was a sound that stilled the restlessness in the room and heightened the anticipation. Then, with quiet grace, the priest entered the room, his robes flowing around him as he took his place at the altar. He nodded gently at the harpist, who continued her soft melody as guests shifted in their seats.

The next moment seemed to stretch out, every detail heightened by the tension in the air. The announcement came, and all eyes turned to the aisle. The groom and best man appeared, walking in step.

Clara's heart skipped a beat. There he was—tall, sharply dressed in a black suit, his face lit with a quiet confidence—a white man. Beside him, the best man, a striking Black man, nodded at familiar faces as they walked forward. The groom reached the altar and stood beside the priest, his eyes fixed on the chapel doors.

Clara, Ifeyinwa, Chinelo, and Ikunnu exchanged shocked glances, their minds racing. *Was this really Chidi?* They could hardly believe it. It seemed almost absurd that Adaobi's groom, the man whose name they'd heard for years, was standing there, a stranger in every sense of the word.

This wasn't the Chidi they had imagined. *Could Adaobi be marrying someone else entirely?* The thought buzzed in their minds like a persistent fly, but there was no denying what was unfolding before them.

"Are we at the wrong wedding?" Ikunnu whispered, her eyes wide with disbelief.

But before anyone could respond, the chapel doors swung open with a soft creak, and all doubts vanished. The announcement was clear: *the bride.* The entire room turned as one, and there, framed in the doorway, was Adaobi.

She was a vision, a bride beyond words. Adaobi's gown was a masterpiece of delicate ivory lace that shimmered with the softest of golden threads. The train of her dress trailed behind her like a whisper, and the bodice fit her like it had been woven from the light itself. Her hair, styled in soft waves, cascaded down her back, crowned with a simple yet elegant veil. The joy in her eyes sparkled like sunlight on water, her smile wide and luminous. Held tenderly on her father's arm, Adaobi seemed to float down the aisle, each step filled with grace, her eyes never leaving the man at the altar.

The friends were momentarily speechless, their hearts swelling with emotion. Whatever doubts or confusion they had before melted away in an instant. They had never seen Adaobi look more beautiful—or more at peace. Her joy was palpable, radiating from her in waves that touched every soul in the room. It didn't matter that the groom wasn't who they expected. What mattered was the love they saw in her eyes, a love so strong that it made the room feel smaller, more intimate, as if the only people who existed were Adaobi and the man waiting for her at the altar.

As she passed, Clara could see it clearly—the happiness, the glow, the pure contentment in Adaobi's expression. It was as if she had stepped into a dream, a dream she had long waited for, and now she was finally living it. Ifeyinwa wiped away a tear, while Chinelo smiled broadly. Ikunnu, always the composed one, gave a quiet nod, her lips curved in a small, approving smile.

There was no doubt now. This was Adaobi's moment, and it was perfect.

"Would you, Edward Giles, take Adaobi Nduka as your wedded wife, to love..."

The words echoed through the small chapel, bouncing off the walls and landing squarely in Clara's ears like a thunderclap. For a split second, the world seemed to stop. Clara's hand instinctively flew to her pregnant belly, her fingers pressing against it as if to steady herself from the shock. She mouthed a silent *"Oh my God"* as her wide eyes flickered between her friends, who looked just as dumbfounded.

Ifeyinwa's jaw dropped slightly, her usual calm demeanor shattered by this unexpected turn of events. Chinelo's eyes widened in disbelief, while Ikunnu sat frozen, blinking rapidly, as if trying to process the words she'd just heard. *Edward Giles? Who was Edward Giles? Weren't they here* to witness Adaobi marry Chidi?

The four friends exchanged glances; their astonishment mirrored in each other's faces. Clara could feel her pulse quicken, a mix of surprise and curiosity rising within her. This wasn't just any plot twist—this was a complete rewrite of everything they thought they knew. Adaobi was never tight-lipped about her relationships, so this was a complete surprise.

When did Chidi become Edward? They all silently wondered. How could Adaobi have kept such a massive change to herself? They had been through so much together—shared secrets, heartbreaks, and dreams of love—yet somehow, this huge revelation had slipped past them.

But as Clara refocused her gaze on the couple standing at the altar, the initial shock began to soften. She saw the way Edward looked at Adaobi, with deep admiration and affection, his eyes never leaving hers. And Adaobi, standing there in her ethereal lace gown, looked more serene and happy than any of them had ever seen her. The way her fingers intertwined with Edward's as they exchanged vows spoke volumes. There was no hesitation, no uncertainty, just pure love.

In that moment, it became clear to the friends that this wasn't a surprise to Adaobi. She knew exactly what she was doing. Adaobi, who had spent years navigating through the uncertainty of romantic relationships, had found her person. Not Chidi, as they had always thought, but Edward. And by the looks of things, Edward adored her.

Clara, still cradling her belly, leaned back slightly and exhaled. Despite the whirlwind of emotions swirling in her mind, a smile began to tug at her lips. If anyone deserved this kind of love, it was Adaobi. Clara looked over at Ifeyinwa, who was wiping a tear from her cheek, and Chinelo, whose shocked expression had softened into a grin. Even Ikunnu, who rarely showed much emotion, nodded approvingly, her eyes glimmering with amusement.

As the priest continued with the vows, the friends relaxed into the moment. Adaobi had certainly thrown them a curveball, but it didn't matter. What mattered was that she had found love—unexpected, yes, but real. And as they watched their dear friend begin the next chapter of her life, the joy in the room became infectious. The shock faded, replaced by happiness for Adaobi and her unexpected love story.

They would hear the full story soon enough, but for now, they were content to witness this beautiful, surprising, and very Adaobi moment.

Acknowledgments

With immense love, gratitude, and respect to my tribe...Agboma Okoroafor, Chike Nzerue, Chukwuma Nwadike, Ifeanyi Samuel Okoroafor, Ikenna Kennedy Okoroafor, Ifeoma Stella Obodo, Ngozi Udom, Chidora Okororie, Eze Ugwueze, Willy Philias, Elsie Dania, Lauretta Akwule, Norah Nzeribe-Windwalker, Obiaku Sylvia Okoroafor, Obiaku Udokamaka Okoronkwo, Uju Oyolu and Ngozi Obikwere-Bell.

---------- Whether by birth or by the beautiful chance of friendship, your unwavering support, boundless wisdom, and deep, unshakable bond have shaped my journey in ways words can barely express. You've stood by me in my brightest moments and carried me through the darkest nights, and for that, I salute each and every one of you. You are my heart's chosen family and my soul's true kin.

Together, we rise higher, dream bigger, and love deeper.

Author Biography

Ejine Okoroafor's journey is one of remarkable ambition and versatility, bridging both the worlds of medicine and literature with a rare and inspiring balance. Born in Nigeria, she began her academic path at the University of Port Harcourt (UniPort) before venturing beyond her home country to study medicine in the former USSR. Her global experiences didn't stop there—after completing her medical training, she relocated to the United Kingdom, where she spent several formative years honing her skills as a doctor before finally settling in the United States, where she is currently based.

As a double-board-certified psychiatrist, Ejine has established herself as a highly respected and dedicated professional in the field of mental health. Her expertise is sought after, and her work in psychiatry has made a meaningful impact on the lives of many patients. However, despite the rigors of her medical career, Ejine has never let go of her deep-seated passion for storytelling, proving that creativity and science can beautifully coexist.

In her writing, she masterfully blends her lived experiences with the rich cultural heritage of Nigeria. Over the years, she has authored an impressive body of work, ranging from novels that dive into the intricacies of human relationships and identity to short story collections, poetry, and children's books.

One of the stories, *Kizito and I,* from her short story collection *Broken Promise and Other Stories,* is currently being adapted into a blockbuster movie. Fans of the gripping tale can soon look forward to seeing it brought to life, either on a popular network or in cinemas near them. The story, known for its compelling narrative and emotional depth, has already generated much anticipation in the literary community, and the film adaptation promises to be a hit with both readers and new audiences alike.

Each of Ejine's literary creations reflects her keen understanding of human emotions, resilience, and the trials that shape people's lives, especially within the context of African culture. Her words are infused with authenticity and empathy, drawing readers into the depths of her characters' struggles and triumphs.

Ejine Okoroafor's journey, both as a psychiatrist and a writer, showcases her indomitable spirit and unwavering commitment to enriching the lives of others—whether through the healing power of medicine or the transformative beauty of storytelling. Her work continues to leave an indelible mark on both fields, affirming her as a trailblazer in her own right.

Books By the Same Author

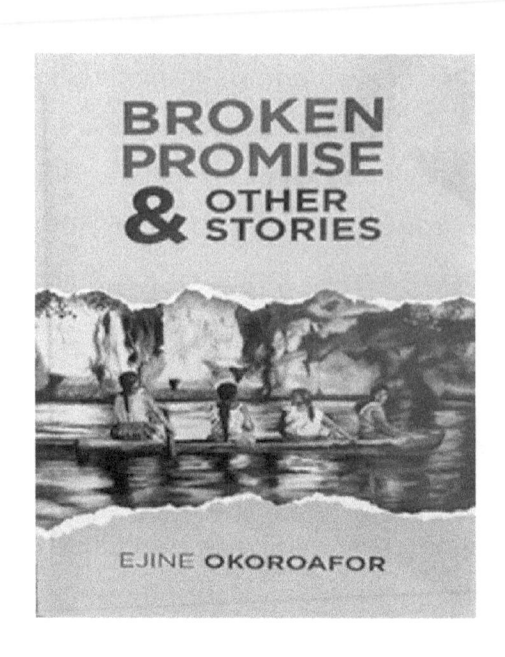

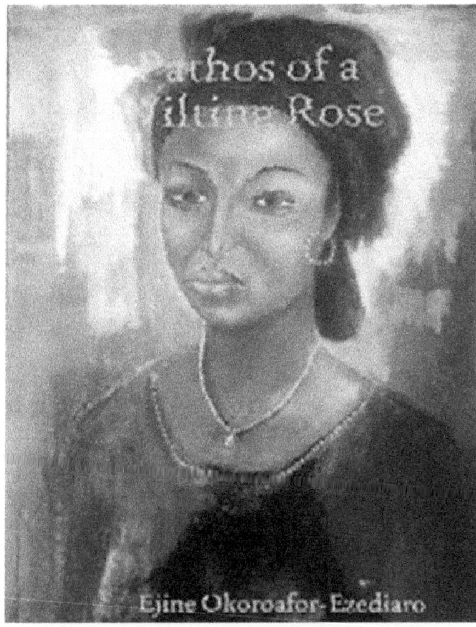
Ejine Okoroafor- Ezediaro

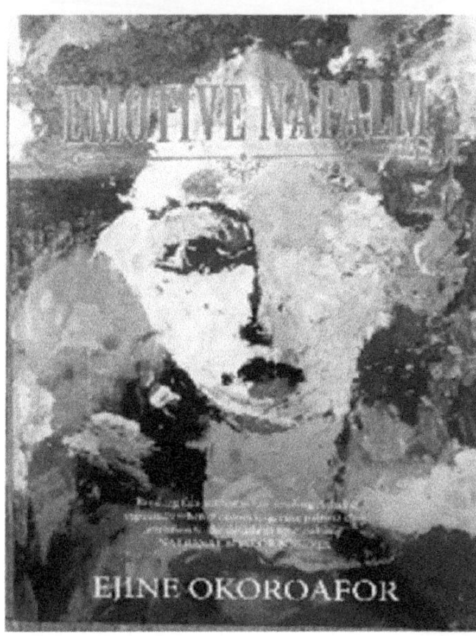
EMOTIVE NAPALM
EJINE OKOROAFOR

Whimsical Rhapsody

Ejine Okoroafor-Ezediaro

INEM'S FOLKLORE SERIES

The Tortoise and the Birds

RETOLD BY
CYNC OKOROAFOR

ILLUSTRATED BY
TOCHUKWU OKOROKWO

(At the Bakery)

By Jane Frances

www.ingramcontent.com/pod-product-compliance
Ingram Content Group UK Ltd.
Pitfield, Milton Keynes, MK11 3LW, UK
UKHW031028171224
452675UK00006B/742